THE URBANA FREE LIBRARY

3 1230 00598 1036

The Urbana Free Library

To renew materials call
217-367-4057

W9-AXG-704

4-05

		DATE DUE		
		DEC 14 2012		

The Spell:
An Extravaganza

Charlotte Brontë

ET REMOTISSIMA PROPE

Hesperus Classics

Hesperus Classics

Published by Hesperus Press Limited

4 Rickett Street, London SW6 1RU

www.hesperuspress.com

First published by Hesperus Press Limited, 2005

Foreword © Nicola Barker, 2005

Designed and typeset by Fraser Muggeridge

Printed in Jordan by Jordan National Press

ISBN: 1-84391-117-5

CONTENTS

We inhabit a world of niches. And it's a wonderful world (just so long, of course, as you're inhabiting the right part of it); it's a shiny, a sensitive and a responsive world. In this world, every object we buy, every design we admire, every game we play, every story we read, is composed and honed and marketed to appeal to its own particular audience. And this audience – this sometimes tiny, often demanding, invariably fastidious audience – is absolutely certain (or fairly certain, at least) that its decision to buy the thing – the book, the shirt, the painting – reflects well on them, that this particular object, this specific *choice* (however small and meagre and trifling), contributes, in some strange and indecipherable way, to an overall definition of who they actually are as Human Beings.

As a people, as a nation, as a *whole*, we are at once strangely fractured by the culture of the niche and yet – and quite paradoxically – deliciously coddled and reassured by it. This may well be because the niche itself has, to all intents and purposes, gradually *become* the culture.

Of course Charlotte Brontë's *The Spell* was written in a different time entirely. This was a time when the niche was merely a small recess into which a statue might be pushed, or a vase, or – and in the Brontë household this was always a strong possibility – it was a place, a nook, into which a shy and wayward sister might suddenly fling herself in order to study her minutely inscribed exercise book of frankly incomprehensible German verbs.

Yet *this* book – this old book, which somehow feels so slippery, so silly, so violent and so young – is all about niches in the most modern of senses. *The Spell* is exclusive. It is cliquish. It is fantastical. It seeks no approval beyond its own.

It is at once singular, smug, fearless and ridiculous. It is deliciously free, yet infuriatingly inaccessible. It is a shared joke told in a quiet sitting room to the flicker of a single candle. You strain to hear the punchline, but you miss it when the fire suddenly crackles and your attention is momentarily distracted. *Damn!*

Later, much later, on finding yourself alone again, you sit and you frown and you ponder. You struggle to solve the riddle. But you don't try too hard (never try *too* hard), because that would be to misunderstand the kind of enterprise this is. That would be to miss out on all the fun and all the silliness.

In essence, then, what makes *The Spell* so right for now – and so exceptional in itself – is that it was composed in a time when, as an aspirant writer, appealing to The Reader always meant appealing to the broadest possible spectrum.

This book was therefore never truly intended for 'Readers' per se. It was only ever meant for friends. And so you should find it as a friend and treat it just as indulgently and just as fondly.

The Spell's magic is that it whisks you into a secret world which you actually have no right to enter – hold your breath! You have no business being here! It beckons you into the smallest and the most elevated of all the world's manifold niches. This book is the tiny, quiet corner where patient Anne and fiery Branwell and grave Emily once sat, and listened, and chuckled – still so young, so green and so full of hope.

This is a flirtatious enterprise. This is Charlotte Brontë utterly without restraint. Her stays are loosed. She is kicking up her heels. Sometimes – and Mrs Gaskell would have rued the day – she even gnashes. This isn't the Charlotte Brontë of legend; the girl and then the woman who worked so hard and cared so deeply and sacrificed so much. This is not the strongly disciplined, stooped-over Charlotte we've all grown up loving, with her careworn dress and terrible eyesight. This is not the creature who 'always showed physical feebleness in everything', who preferred to stand in the shade and eschew the sun.

The Spell is the writer *before* the writing. This is The Artist before The Life began to impinge on her Art, before necessity tapped her, chipped her and nudged her into all kinds of improbable positions, before it taught her the lessons which we've all dutifully learnt – from the great poise and wisdom of her pen – in her stead.

This book is more Theatre than Writing, more sadistic than loving, more cruel than gentle. And above all else, what it shows us (and it's an essential thing), is how *alike* those two astonishing sisters were, not how different; how Charlotte *was* Emily (pugnacious, roving, excessive, untamed) before the pressures of life shaped her into the Guard, the Protector, the Wife and the Mother.

'I have some qualities,' Charlotte once wrote (not long after *The Spell* was wrought), 'that make me very miserable, some feelings that you can have no participation in – that few, very few, people in the world can at all understand. I don't pride myself on these peculiarities. I strive to conceal and suppress them as much as I can; but they burst out sometimes…'

The Spell – this funny yet immodestly *modest* enterprise – is a tiny, perfectly captivating part of that bursting.

– *Nicola Barker, 2005*

The quotations cited above are taken from *The Life of Charlotte Brontë* by Elizabeth Gaskell (Penguin, 1997).

The Spell

Duke of Wellington

Duke of Zamorna [Arthur Augustus Adrian Wellesley], *Marquis of Douro and King of Angria, son of the Duke of Wellington*

Marquis of Almeida [Arthur Julius Wellesley], *infant son of Zamorna, deceased*

Florence Marian Wellesley, *former wife of Zamorna and mother of the Marquis of Almeida, deceased*

Duchess of Zamorna [Mary Henrietta Wellesley], *wife of Zamorna, daughter of the Earl of Northangerland*

Lord Charles Albert Florian Wellesley, *narrator and younger brother of Zamorna*

Countess Seymour [Lady Isabella Wellesley], *aunt of Zamorna*

Earl of Seymour, *husband of the Countess Seymour*

Lord Fitzroy, *son of the Countess Seymour*

Cecillia, Eliza, Georgiana, Catharine, Agnes and Helen, *daughters of the Countess Seymour*

Marchioness Louisa, *aunt of Zamorna*

Julia Sydney, *cousin of Zamorna*

Edward Sydney [Prince of York], *husband of Julia Wellesley*

Lady Helen Percy, *grandmother of the Duchess of Zamorna*

Earl of Northangerland, [Alexander Percy], *father-in-law of Zamorna*

Lady Zenobia Ellrington, *wife of the Earl of Northangerland; stepmother-in-law of Zamorna*

Edward Percy, *eldest son of the Earl of Northangerland; brother-in-law and aide-de-camp to Zamorna*

Maria Percy [Princess Mary Sneachie], *wife of Edward Percy*

William Percy, *son of the Earl of Northangerland; brother-in-law to Zamorna*

Duchess of Valdecella [Emily Inez], *Marchioness of Alhamas*

Lord Ernest Edward Fitz-Arthur Ravenswood Wellesley, *son of the Duchess of Valdacella*

Lady Emily Augusta Wellesley, *daughter of the Duchess of Valdacella*

Duke of Fidena [John Augustus Sneachie], *Prince of Sneachisland*

Duchess of Fidena [Lily Hart], *wife of the Duke of Fidena*

Marquis of Rossendale [John Augustus], *son of the Duke of Fidena*

Lady Isidore Hume, *mother of Florence Marian and former mother-in-law of Zamorna*

Lady Frances Millicent Hume, *daughter of Lady Isidore Hume*

Euphemia Lindsay, *protégé to Lady Frances Millicent Hume*

Dr Alford, *Physician-in-ordinary to Zamorna*

Dr Stanhope, *Primate of Angria*

Mr Sumner, Mr Abercrombie and Sir Astley Coleridge, *doctors*

Mr Montmorency, Mr Warner, Viscount Castlereagh and the Earl of Arundel, *Verdopolitan noblemen*

General Thornton, *guardian to Charles Wellesley*

Eugene Rosier, *page to Zamorna*

Finic, *Zamorna's mute dwarf servant*

Mina Laury, *nurse*

Edward Laury, *Zamorna's valet, father of Mina Laury*

William Maxwell, *steward of Zamorna*

Annabel Temple, *housekeeper of Zamorna*

Roland and Roswal, *Zamorna's dogs*

PREFACE

The Duke of Zamorna should not have excluded me from Wellesley House, for the following pages have been the result of that exclusion. Does he think I can patiently bear to be wholly separated from my sister-in-law, a lady whom I love and honour more than any other in Verdopolis? Does he think I can calmly endure that she, by his orders, should turn from me if I chance to meet her in public places, and when I beg a seat in her carriage that she should, smiling and shaking her head, deny me with sweet reluctance and – the unkindest cut of all – offer me the indignity of ordering a footman to remove me when I commence, by tears and cries, to give vent to my indignation in the open street? I say, does he think I am to lie down like a flogged spaniel under all this?

If such are his ideas, let him be undeceived. Here I fling him my revenge. He will not like the morsel. In this book I have tampered with his heartstrings. Perhaps a casual spectator may think that he is highly flattered and so forth – the tale, part of it at least, being told by his own wife – but to him the whole affair will be unendurable. There are passages of truth here which will make him gnash his teeth with grating agony. I am not at liberty to point out what those passages are, but he will discover them, and he will know thereby that there is one person at least in Verdopolis thoroughly acquainted with all the depths, false or true, of his double-dealing, hypocritical, close, dark, secret, half-insane character.

Serfs of Angria! Freemen of Verdopolis! I tell you that your tyrant and your idol is mad! Yes, there are black veins of utter perversion of intellect born with him and running through his whole soul. He acts at times under the control of impulses that he cannot resist; displays all the strange variableness and versatility which characterise possessed lunatics; runs head-strong forwards in dark bypaths sharply angular from the straight road of common use and custom; and is, in short, an ungovernable, fiery fool.

All this is declared in my present work rather by implication than assertion. The reader will find here no lengthened passage which elaborately sets forth his outrageous peculiarities. He must gather it from the hints interwoven with the whole surface and progress of the story. When he has finished, let him shut the book and, dismissing from his mind every fictitious circumstance, let him choose such only as have self-evident marks of reality about them. Then, after due consideration, let him deliver his opinion. Is the Duke of Zamorna sane or insane? This question I leave to his decision and in the meantime with acknowledgements for past and prayers for future favours,

I remain the public's obedient servant,

C.A.F. Wellesley[1]

CHAPTER ONE

The young Marquis of Almeida is dead. This everybody knows. He has left the inheritance of two thrones vacant. Wellingtonsland and Angria now wait for an heir.

Inexorable death! All the guards and precautions that the royal Zamorna could put about his first born, his darling, the first hope of *his* kingdom and the second of his father's, were unable to withstand that scythe whose keen edge alike destroys the withered, the full-blown and the budding flower.

In vain were the obsequious attentions of a hundred servants, the utmost exertions of scientific skill, the maternal care of Mina Laury, whose tenderness once raised the father but could not raise the son to life, the shrine-like solitude of the lone manor house, the balmy airs of health breathed over its antique woods and scented dells and rushing, rapid rivulet. And lastly, wholly vain was the energetic wish which, till it was quenched in despair, continually filled Zamorna's soul that he – whom he loved with an affection past the power of words to express, because he was the only son of his mother – might live and flourish to remind him of the departed. He died, cut off early, called away before he knew what the world was, over whose expanse his morning had risen so fairly.

The Duke sent Lord Julius from his presence, that parental anxiety, strained and tortured by the evident delicacy of the plant it watched, might not become rather a check to, than an encourager of its welfare. I know when the grave closed on Marian, a nervous dread took possession of his mind lest the seeds of the mother's malady might have been transmitted with existence to the child. He hated to look at its brightly tinted cheek and sparkling eyes, its beautifully turned limbs, and the white clear complexion beneath which veins and even arteries might be seen meandering in wavy lines of the faintest and finest violet. I have often heard him groan and curse on the beauty which to him brought thoughts only of unmingled bitterness, as with a heart-wrung sigh he has laid down the exquisite miniature of his own grand image, after gazing on it for a few brief moments of evanescent, and, as he too well felt, unfounded exultation. 'What would I give,' he has muttered on such occasions, 'if my son had a little, a very little less of his mother's delicate loveliness. Oh, I abhor now, with my whole soul, every touch of beauty which appears too ethereal for humanity; every shade in the colour of a cheek, every ray in the light of an eye that has too much of the heavenly, too little of the earthly, even every inflection of a voice whose sweetness goes to the heart with a sudden thrill is now to me not a cause of delight but agony.'

When the first letter came from Grassmere, intimating that the ineradicable upas tree of consumption had begun to put forth its shoots, he exclaimed (for I was in the room, of course unknown to him, while he perused it), 'I knew it would be so! I'm almost glad the horrors of suspense are past! I need not tamper with hope, now there is a clear unblocked path of certainty. He lingers for a few months, perhaps weeks. Aye, Florence was only eight weeks in dying. And then he finds a resting place in that accursed vault. Yet I wish it was *all* over, sickness, death, burial and all! Then I might be satisfied, if not happy, but *till* then –' He threw himself into a chair which stood near his desk, tore out a sheet of paper, and, with the rapidity of lightning, dashed down the following lines:

My priceless Mina,
Your work is nearly completed. It has been a hard task to preserve what destiny had marked for decay. I know how you

have discharged it. With my own lips I will hereafter declare my approbation. Watch a few days and nights longer. Just see that the last pulse has vibrated and the last breath exhaled. Then, my girl, rest from your labours. Let me hear nothing from you, not one word, not one syllable, till you think the scene is about finally to close, when he seems to have no more than perhaps a week's strength in him, that is to say, my girl, when respiration begins to rattle in his throat and the infernal brightness dies off his cheek, and his flesh (the little that remains) grows perfectly transparent, showing no blood, but bones. These things having come to pass, you may write and tell me. I'll annihilate the interval, if possible.

Farewell, my sweet wild rose! Your beauty will, I fear, be faded by deathbed vigils before I next see you. Never mind, I care not for that, and if my heart and my love be yours, I know that Mina Laury thinks little of the light – favourable or unfavourable – in which the rest of the world may behold her. Faithful till death (thine or mine I mean, girl, not intermediate ones, they seem to be coming thick), I am and shall ever be,

Your own Zamorna

Such was the reply he sent to poor Mina's timid and apprehensive epistle. A strange one! So at least I thought. He sealed and directed it, then ordered his carriage and left Verdopolis for Angria.[2]

Nothing could exceed the restless activity and irritable violence which marked his conduct during the next five or six weeks. He is always energetic, always passionately eager in any course he pursues. Ever since I knew him it has been his custom to give up heart and soul to the furtherance of a favourite plan, but now he seemed to give up life also.

Even Warner could scarcely keep pace with him. He plunged impetuously into the thick of business, sought after the most thronging employment with intense solicitude, but yet hardly appeared to feel pleasure in it when it was found. All day long he might be seen walking through the unpaved streets of Adrianopolis, watching and actively superintending the labours of the toiling workmen, now directing the construction of an arch, now the craning up of some vast block of stone or marble, standing amidst the din and tumult of uncreated squares and terraces, whilst the deep foundations of future mansions were dug in the stubborn soil.

Everywhere the tall figure of the slender youth, in his close black dress and unornamental cap thickly cinctured with curls, might be seen passing along with commanding tread and bearing, controlling all around him like the sovereign spirit of the storm. Sometimes that shape appeared lofty against the sky, standing on a thread-like scaffolding, a blue abyss of air on each side, before and behind the skeleton erection of an unfinished palace, honeycombed with arches, and vast beams flung across as the divisions of state chambers, between voids that might turn the head of a cabin boy giddy. And here the monarch walked as fearlessly as an eagle hangs, poised above his eyrie. The eyes of his stern and swarthy subjects were often turned admiringly on him as he sprung like a young elk from one narrow projection to another, and strode over the shaking beams as erectly and haughtily as if he were crossing a hall of Wellesley House. At other times the eye might single him out, overtopping a throng of subordinates, gathered round the pit of some half-sunk foundation, watching intently while a train was laid to blast the rocks beneath, and, when the whole infernal disposition was completed, giving the order to fall back in his own full and thrilling tones, lingering the last on the path of retreat, and, as the heaven-rending thunder burst up from its stony tomb in a crack that shook hill and plain, far and near, commencing the triumphant huzza, whose swell arose as the peal of the rock-quake died into groaning echoes. But when all this was past, towards evening, when the workmen had retired from the busy scene, when the architects and master masons and carpenters had gathered together their rules, squares, compasses, etc., and departed, then might a spectator, if any at that time tarried on the scene, discern that stately form sitting solitary on the rough-hewn steps of an embryo hall. All around him silent, lonely, desolate. Still as Tadmor in the wilderness, voiceless as Tyre on the forsaken sea.[3] Mallet, hammer, axe and chisel all unheard. The blast-thunder of the day forgotten, the shouts of the labourers asleep, their echoing footsteps passed away, and the lull of twilight stealing on a faint wind, and the low moan of the old inhabited town down from heaven, up from earth, through the becalmed region. At such an hour Zamorna's figure would be visible, sole inhabitant of his rising city, his arms probably folded on his breast; his eyes fixed with a mingled expression of thought and vigilance (not much of sorrow) on the yellow prairie stretching eastward before him, and finding no boundary save the golden skyline; the brow of youth and beauty, clothed with a cloud of sternness that lay on it as the shadow of an ominous sky lies on the white marble wall of a palace; the fresh red lips closely met, as placidly motionless as if eternal silence had fixed them with her seal, and no token of deep emotion apparent, of any feeling, indeed, save absorbing meditation, except the varying hue of the cheek, which now and then, at long intervals, died suddenly away from its ordinary warm bright flush to a stricken and colourless pallor. Then it might be known there was a worm gnawing at the heart, that some pang, of deadlier agony than usual, had called the blood back to its source. But ere long the pure eloquent glow would steal again over the whitened complexion, and as the Duke slightly changed his position and turned his eyes more fixedly to the dim east, or perhaps let them fall on the reedy banks of the Calabar[4], it was evident his spirit had, for a time at least, conquered its inward tormentor, and that plans of warlike or political ambition were once more forced into predominance over the paternal anguish whose recurrence racked him so bitterly.

He was sitting thus one evening when a step echoed through the silent square, and Eugene Rosier advanced from the long shadows of the surrounding buildings.

'Hah!' said his master, rising up and going forward to meet him. 'Hah, Eugene! Are they come?'

'Yes, my lord, last night at ten o'clock. There were three carriages only: Miss Laury and Mr Sydney, the mourning coach with the corpse, and the undertaker's barouche.'

'Eugene, enough! But where are Ernest and Emily, and – and, you understand me, sir – *the others*.' This was spoken with emphasis.

Eugene bowed. 'I believe they follow tomorrow, my lord,' he replied. 'His Grace went to meet them as far as Free Town.'

'His Grace! What! The Duke has been here then?'

'Yes, my lord, for the last four weeks, but not at Wellesley House.'

'I wonder I have not seen him.'

'He feared a collision; the Angrian road is so public.'

Zamorna now bent his face low and sternly laid his hand on Rosier's shoulder.

'You say,' he muttered in a suppressed tone, 'that he has been *about* Verdopolis four weeks. Has Finic watched?'

'Aye, my lord, like a lynx, and so have I, but there was little occasion. He is circumspect in his ways.'

'Good,' said the Duke, drawing himself up. 'I am satisfied, for I imagine I can depend on *you*; at least if I thought a moment otherwise –' He paused and directed an awfully piercing glance on the page, who stood it manfully.

'I speak the truth to you, my lord,' he said, 'for I know a lie, on that subject especially, would inevitably bring me sooner or later to the fiery draught and leaden pill. Besides, circumstances bear testimony in my favour. He dare not take the slightest advantage if he would, for he knows how grandly Your Grace could retaliate.' Rosier concluded with a slight laugh, and a sly look of his ineffably mischievous eye.

'Silence!' said Zamorna, in tones nearly as deep as smothered thunder. 'How dare you jest with me, sir? I have no wish to retaliate. Retaliate! No, if he gave me cause to *retaliate*, the matter would be all up. His life or mine would then be the only admissible cards in the great game we have so long played together. How and when will it end? I wish the stakes were swept away, by whose hands I care not.'

'By the hand that first flung them down,' muttered another voice, as deep in its inflections as Zamorna's own, but instead of the full harmony which lingers in every word that falls from his lips, a discordant harshness now grated on the ear.

The Duke did not appear startled by this sudden interruption. He answered calmly, without turning round, 'Aye, that would be the fittest for the work. But, my old friend, come forwards. I know your tongue, let us see your face. You need not fear intruders, unless a bat or a night heron be reckoned as such.'

'Few of those, I take it, remain *now* among the reeds of the Calabar,' replied the same voice, and a dark figure stole from behind a vast pile of mortar and stood confronting Zamorna.

'Very few,' was the reply. 'Spade, mattock and builder's axe have rung so loud a warning to the old settlers on that plain and on those rushy shores that scarce a wing is left now to wave between us and the horizon.'

'Spade and mattock are ringing a warning elsewhere,' replied the stranger. 'There's a grave dug in Verdopolis tonight.'

'There's a vault opened,' said the Duke. 'How does the bed-rat's lantern shine in that dim subterranean aisle, and in what fashion does the key agree with its rusty wards?'

'The bed-rat's lantern shines bravely,' returned he, 'and it is glancing on the golden plates of three princely coffins. Should there not be room made for a fourth? The key turns as if the underground damps had oiled instead of hardening it, and the grave will unfold tomorrow night as noiselessly as if the sick, instead of the dead, lay within its bars. But Zamorna, where must the child lie?'

'On its mother's bosom,' replied Zamorna, in sternly suppressed accents.

'Aye, and you must lay it there. She'd turn in her coffin if any other hand performed that office, Duke. Will there be any other mourners at the funeral?'

'Few, I think. Tears fall scantily over a corpse of six months old.'

'So much the better. Let me reckon the tale of those likely to be present.'

'Have done with the subject!' exclaimed Zamorna, in a tone of sudden passion, which, till now, he had restrained, either through respect or some other cause.

'I will when it pleases me,' replied his friend. 'My young lord, you'll of course see your wife on the occasion of visiting her residence; only a thin plank of cedar and a covering of velvet will interpose between her and you. Lift them up, and the Lady Florence, the pride of the west, lies there in all her charms. Nay, not all, she's somewhat faded and wasted, it must be allowed, but if the eye be quenched, the cheek turned to clay, and the features forever obliterated, what does that matter to her kindly husband? He is far too faithful to love her the less for any slight failure in that beauty which he once thought matchless.'

A muttered but horrible curse broke from the Duke's lips in reply to this sarcasm. It was met by the low, inward laugh of the stranger, and he went on: 'Truly, Monarch, I shall marvel if you neglect to speak with her face to face. *She* did not shrink from *you* when she placed your first born in your arms, and why should *you* from *her* when you return that kind office? Ah, she'll look sadly at her Arthur and moan to herself when he is gone, as she did that night on leaving the Gladiator's Hall. You heard her then, but would not take pity, so she sat down in silence to fulfil her destiny, dree her weird[5].'

There was a pause. Zamorna stood leaning against an upright block of stone. The light of a broad yellow moon, which was now hanging high in the placid heavens, fell full on him, and defined features as white as those of a sheeted ghost. His face was utterly bloodless, and the dark curls clustering on his forehead and temples contrasted ghastlily with the spectral paleness of what they shadowed. His eyes looked rather upwards; they were not dim with tears, but glittering with fiery defiance. The rest of his countenance was calm; it seemed as if he could overmaster the deadly and burning rage which filled him except where transparency showed the smothered flame flashing fiercely through.

'Have you done?' he at last asked after some minutes of mutual silence.

'Yes,' said the stranger. 'I've given you a large enough dose for the present. You may digest it at your leisure. Remember that long "moan" of stricken anguish, which nearly made you repent and turn back on your path?'

'I do remember it,' said the Duke, and at the same moment he smiled. 'I remember it well, but you are mistaken, sir, if you think it made me repent, and you are mistaken still more in saying that I would not take pity on Marian's distress. The distress gratified my pride, sir, and therefore, be sure, it changed both my love and compassion, and, unless your sagacity is much at fault, you know that I told her so, and that I spent five hours of that night in reasoning with and consoling her. The dawn of the next day found her calm and resigned, almost happy, for she knew that my affection was totally unchanged, that I loved her as well as ever, and that it was that very love which caused me to take the step I had then determined on. For if I had permitted her to remain an impediment to my inclinations, I should soon have hated her – lovely, devoted and innocent as she was – and my blood was cold at the bare imagination of that.'

'Well,' interrupted the stranger, 'these things you alleged, I suppose, in justification of your conduct.'

'Not in justification, sir. I never justified myself to any woman breathing! But I employed that reason as a means of comforting her and, I am proud to say, not without effect, for when the morning light glimmered through the window, in whose recess she sat for the last time by my side, it fell upon a face as placid and resigned as, a few hours before, it had been inexpressibly sad and mournful. I had wiped away all her tears. Though there was melancholy in the smile, which my final embrace called to her sweet features, there was no misery.

Sir, you think I am a prey to remorse. Be undeceived, I know not what remorse is!'

'A lie! A lie!' said the unknown. 'Your heart is now torn with it! That subdued voice and ashy countenance give signs of a worm that will not die! Don't think to deceive me, Zamorna! I know you too well.'

'Yet not well enough,' replied the Duke, 'or you would know the change in my voice and countenance is owing to hatred of yourself rather than regret for either my wife or son. I loved them both with a deeper love than words can express. Their untimely removal has, I confess, inflicted a wound that the lapse of centuries can never entirely heal, but, sir, abhorrence is stronger than grief in its sternest form, and though there may be moments, even hours, in my life when I shall forget to lament the dead, there will never be an instant when I shall cease to regard you with the bitterest detestation.'

A low malignant laugh was the stranger's only answer. He folded more closely round him the cloak in which he was enveloped, nodded to Zamorna, and gliding across the square, was quickly lost to sight.

'Hah!' said the Duke, when he was gone. 'I wish the wretch had stayed one minute longer. Though I loathe his presence so intensely, I would yet have detained him to ask what issue events are drawing to. The mystery contained in those lines I have so often heard in my infancy, and *once* since manhood's sun shone fervidly on my path, seems unfolding.

> '*When the wave of death's river*
> 　*Hides the rose in its bloom,*
> *When the gift and the giver*
> 　*Lie low in the tomb,*
> 　*When the fresh fruit is shaken,*

The bright blossoms blown,
When the flower falls forsaken
And withered and lone,
Then upwards to heaven
The dim cloud shall swell,
The veil shall be riven
And broken the spell.

'There is more, but I forget it. Well, time is the great revealer of secrets, and no hand can delay its progress, yet it seems the sacrifice has been exacted from me and me alone. My flower and fruit are gone, while *his* – Good God! I am not going to wish their death, am I! No, no, that would be a black addition to the mutual pile of affliction, more tears to be wrung from a heart that has few to spare; his, I think, would weep blood. I likewise should desire no third overshadowing of death even on that side. The cloud which has now fallen will be long ere it dissipate. Oh! Florence! Florence! My sky can never again shine as brightly as it has done. There is a continual dimness round the horizon which *will not* pass away.'

In bitter melancholy he paced the square and, except the sound of his measured footsteps, all was unbroken silence for the next quarter of an hour. At the end of that time he paused.

'Eugene,' said he, 'come, I shall leave Adrianopolis immediately. My presence at Douro Villa will, I dare say, be much missed, especially if the mourners are late in arriving. You said that *he* was expected *tomorrow*, did you not?'

Eugene answered in the affirmative, and page and master departed together.

CHAPTER TWO

On the subsequent evening, or rather night, a message arrived from my father summoning me instantly to Waterloo Palace. I was in bed when the servant arrived, for it was near eleven o'clock, but I rose instantly, and, as soon as I was dressed, hastened to obey the mandate.

On entering the north drawing room, where a footman informed me the Duke awaited my arrival, I found him seated with a lady whom I presently recognised as my aunt, the Countess Seymour. Both she and my father were dressed in deep mourning, and an air of thoughtful solemnity brooded on the brow of each. I came up to the hearth and, warming my hands at the red bright fire, for it was a somewhat chilly night, I asked, 'Is the funeral to take place this evening?'

'The funeral!' exclaimed Lady Seymour. 'Child, how did you know of the death or even sickness? Augustus has been as secret and uncommunicative as ever during the progress of the whole affair.'

'Aye, but it would be difficult for him to be *so* secret that *I* should not find him out. There are not above two or three incidents of his life which are unknown to me, and one of these must have happened before I was born.'

'Well,' said my father, 'be that as it may, your penetration has hit the mark this time. Charles, your nephew, Lord Almeida, has been dead upwards of a week. He will be buried in an hour's time. If you will solemnly promise to restrain that prying curiosity of yours which has already given your brother so much inconvenience, I may permit you to attend the funeral. But if your elfish disposition will not allow the fulfilment of such a condition, stay at home. I have no wish to subject you to any painful restraint.'

I readily promised, and then proceeded to ask my father why this discretion was so requisite.

'There will be persons there,' he said, 'whom you never saw before. It is my pleasure that you should not yet become acquainted with them, for reasons which, with all your precocity, sir, you would find a difficulty yet in comprehending. So make not the slightest attempt to discover their identity either by word, look, or sign. My severe displeasure will be the reward of disobedience.'

Again I promised, but I could not help wondering who these prohibited personages might be.

'Isabella,' continued my father, addressing Lady Seymour, '*you* will take charge of him. Keep his hand fast clasped in your own, and do not let him leave your side one instant till the ceremony is over and the mourners gone.'

'I shall be careful, Brother,' replied my aunt. 'For were Augustus – in his present dark and bitter mood – to notice even a prying look in his face, the consequences might be fatal.'

'He must not come *near* Augustus!' replied my father sternly. 'I will hazard neither his life nor that of the others. And they are so sudden and dangerous on that point, while he is so incurably inquisitive, that assuredly in case of collision the sequel would be a tragic one.' My father now struck his gold repeater. 'It is half-past eleven, and I hear them bringing the carriage round to the private door. Come, Isabella, there is no time for delay.'

He took up his craped hat and black gloves, which lay on a sideboard and, drawing my aunt's arm through his, led her from the room and down the grand staircase. The carriage was drawn up close under the portico, for the night was very wild and wet. Both entered. I was lifted in after by a servant; my father took me on his knee and we drove off.

Notwithstanding the noise of the wheels, the bustle of the streets around, the howling of the wind, and the incessant clattering of the rain, I fell fast asleep in my comfortable position and awoke only when the motion of the carriage ceased. We had stopped under St Michael's. As we alighted, the great doors flew open to admit us and closed directly behind. All within was silent, lonely, and, but for the gleam of two solitary lamps, would have been shrouded in utter darkness. One of these glinted dimly from behind the curtain of the organ gallery, and the other was carried by the verger who let us in. This man wore his official stole and his face was masked.

'Are they come?' asked the Duke of Wellington.

'Yes, my lord, they are all assembled in the burial aisle.'

'Lead the way, then,' continued His Grace.

The verger obeyed and, taking his lamp, glided on before us as we passed under the grand dome, whose vast altitude was now unseen in the thick darkness that filled the cathedral. A low note stole from the organ. As it died away others followed, and soon a requiem of Mozart's swelled with subduing solemnity through the whole void of pitch-dark air. I paused to listen. Lady Seymour seized my hand and hurried me forwards without speaking. We stopped at the door leading to the royal burial aisle of the Wellesleys. Our conductor tapped; it was opened from within and we entered. Many lamps were burning in the house of death, but all with a dim and discoloured flame, as if they loathed the air that fanned them. The vaulted walls were clearly seen. They looked dark and damp, but not slimy. Many niches were formed in them for the reception of coffins and three of these were occupied. A sepulchral urn stood before each. The centre of the aisle was occupied by a bier supporting a small coffin covered with a pall of white velvet. Round this were ranged the mourners. I obtained a full view of all as I entered, and the following is the most correct description I can give.

Dr Stanhope, the Primate of Angria, stood at the head, gowned and cassocked. At his right hand, Mr Sumner in plain mourning, at his left Dr Alford, ditto. A little in the background and leaning against the wall with his arms folded, and his eyes fixed intently on the ground, appeared Zamorna, as pale and motionless as if he too had been an image of lifeless mortality. No tear trembled in the long dark lashes that reposed on his cheek, and his brow, as usual, wore an aspect more of sternness than sorrow. Close beside him stood Mina Laury. Her face and her whole person turned, I believe unconsciously, rather away from the general group and towards him. She wept much, but her tears flowed freest after she had looked at the pale face of the lofty figure standing near her.

Opposite was Ernest Fitz-Arthur. His countenance was covered with his hands; drops trickled through his fingers; but, actuated by the same spirit as his father, he was too proud to give way to any more audible expression of his grief. He has remarkably warm and ardent feelings for one so young. And I saw it was a hard struggle to suppress the sorrow with which his heart was heaving. So far all the mourners were known to me, but at the foot of the bier were placed two with whom I was unacquainted. A lady and a gentleman, the former shrouded in a double veil of black crape, the latter in a cloak of sables. They whispered now and then to each other very low, and once the lady stepped up to Zamorna. She spoke in a soothing tone. He smiled faintly and told her to speak to that child, pointing to Ernest, 'if she wished to comfort the afflicted'.

'No,' was her reply. 'Edward ought to weep, his playmate's death has been a heavy loss to him. But for you, his removal may on the whole be rather a mercy than otherwise.'

'Well, Emily,' returned he, 'you see no tear on my cheek. Poor Mina,' and he turned to her with a look of compassion, 'is sorry for her nursling, but I am as calm as –' He directed a significant glance to the figure in sables before alluded to and paused.

'Calm, Augustus!' said the lady. 'Aye, outside, but you look so deadly white.'

'Emily,' said the Duke, 'lift up his mantle and see whether he too does not look white?'

She shook her head and moved away.

My father now came forwards. He advanced to the two strangers; the gentleman held out his hand, which His Grace of Wellington grasped most warmly. The lady put aside her veil, but as she, at that moment, turned her back to me, her features remained as much a mystery as ever. The Duke saluted her on the forehead in silence. He and the masculine incognito then moved away to a little distance. For some time they continued to walk in the further part of the aisle, conversing earnestly in subdued whispers. I could now see that the step and bearing of the stranger were remarkably noble, his stature was lofty, and his voice, repressed as it was, sounded deep and commanding.

Ere long the vault door reopened and, marshalled by the masked verger, Prince John of Sneachisland entered; Lord Rossendale accompanied him. Both were, of course, attired in black. Rossendale took his station by Ernest. He regarded him with an expression of frank-hearted sympathy, but said nothing. Fitz-Arthur dashed away his tears the moment his friend entered, and, biting his lip, seemed resolved to show no more weakness. Fidena passed by Zamorna without observing him, for, as I have already said, Arthur stood a little aloof. He walked to my father and his companion and, bowing to the former, was about to take the latter's hand, saying, 'My dear Zamorna, how are you?'

A passionate and haughty repulse made him fall back a step or two. He looked round with surprise. Arthur strode hastily up to him. His face, which a moment before had been cold and colourless as marble, glowed like scarlet.

'John,' said he, convulsively grasping his arm, 'do you not know me?'

'Certainly, Arthur, I do, but for the moment not perceiving you, and observing a tall gentleman with your father, I was led into a mistake. It is now, however, rectified, and as no offence was intended, so I trust none has been taken.'

The stranger, without reply and keeping his face still muffled in the shrouding cloak, resumed his station by the veiled lady.

Zamorna pressed Fidena's hand in both his, and an interval of deep silence ensued. It was broken by the grating sound of the vault key as the vergers turned it in the rusty wards.

'Are all here?' asked the Duke of Wellington, observing this action.

'All,' was the concise reply of Zamorna.

'Stanhope, commence the service,' continued His Grace.

The book was laid open, and the solemnly impressive voice of the primate soon echoed through the aisle as it consigned to dust and corruption those cold remains which the canopy of the pall and the gilded planks of the coffin alone concealed from our sight. The awful words were said: he had committed earth to earth, ashes to ashes.[6] The corpse was placed in its appropriate niche, and far off we heard the long stealing chords of the organ, and the softened voices of the choristers as they joined in that grand and thrilling chant, 'I know that my Redeemer liveth'[7]. These sounds passed mournfully away, but as they died, another burst in thunder above us. It was the great bell of St Michael's, whose deep-struck toll, now clanging from its domed elevation, announced to all Verdopolis that the young heir of Angria and Wellingtonsland was laid at rest in the last home of his royal kindred. Few tears fell on the coffin of the infant prince. None from the eye of his father, none from that of his grandfather, of his uncle of Fidena, of the strangers. Mina wept, as Zamorna said, for her nursling, and Fitz-Arthur for his playmate, but beside these the inheritor of two thrones could command no single tribute of regret from all his thousand future subjects.

All were about to quit the vault when the verger stepped forwards. He placed one hand on the empty bier, and rolling his eyes, which glittered like steel within the mask, over the group of mourners, he said in the deep harsh tones I had heard last night two hundred miles off:

> '*The wave of death's river*
>   *Hides the rose in its bloom,*
> *The gift and the giver*
>   *Sleep low in the tomb,*
> *The fresh fruit is shaken,*
>   *The bright blossom strown,*
> *The flower lies forsaken*
>   *And withered and lone.*
> *Then upward to heaven*
>   *The dim cloud shall swell,*
> *The veil shall be riven*
>   *And broken the spell.*

But slowly the cloud must rise,
　　Faint is the gale
That sighs through the muffled skies,
　　Breathes on the veil.
High was the wanderer's power,
　　Wondrous his spell,
It wrought in their natal hour
　　Strongly and well.
A might is yet on them
　　No mortal can quell,
A charm rests upon them
　　Which none can dispel,
The watch through the dark time of star and of shade,
　　The shadow shall vanish, the starlight shall fade.'

Not one of those present looked astonished at this strange incident. Stanhope and Sumner whispered together, and Fidena muttered, 'Hah, I have heard something of this.' The rest were evidently fully acquainted with the whole mystery of the business.

All now left the vault and, lit on their path by the verger, proceeded through the dark and silent cathedral to their carriages. Mina, the veiled lady and Ernest Fitz-Arthur were handed by Zamorna into his. He entered after them and they drove off. Fidena and Rossendale then departed, and the Duke of Wellington, Lady Seymour and myself remained alone with the stranger. He spoke a few words aside to the Duke in that low and very sweet tone he had used all along. He then offered his arm to my aunt. She accepted it willingly enough, and he handed her into the carriage. My father entered next, and left me standing close to the stranger.

I felt an odd kind of thrill run through me as he suddenly bent down his stately figure, and, taking me in his arms, lifted me onto the carriage seat. He followed, placed himself beside me, and as the horses whipped off, I felt his hand, evidently a small and slender-fingered one, laid on mine with a gentle pressure. The touch electrified me. I screamed out.

'Heavens!' said my aunt in a tone of terror.

'Good God!' exclaimed my father in one of anger. 'What are you doing, sir? You must be aware of the elf's disposition! Don't lay a finger on him! He would find you out by one of your hands.'

The stranger laughed slightly, and, drawing himself a little from me, he leant his head against the side of the carriage.

'Find him out by one of his hands,' repeated I to myself. Aye, there was something peculiar in that hand, something very insinuating in the feel of its warm, slight fingers, and I think familiar. I have felt them before. If I could only touch his face now – his head – it would help me to guess. I'll try. He seems not ill-disposed towards me.

I began noiselessly to creep to his side. Already my hand had penetrated the folds of the muffling cloak; my finger touched his forehead. He started as if adder stung, and the next moment I was stretched senseless in the bottom of the carriage.

On awaking from this dream the mild face of Lady Seymour was the first object that met my eyes. She was bending over me and my head rested on her knee. A magnificent apartment was above and around me, and the pure lustre of shaded lights slept on the walls and ceiling.

'Aunt,' said I, 'where am I?'

'In my house, Charles, in Seymour Place. Don't look so startled, child, there are none but friends round you.'

I gazed about wildly enough, I suppose in search of the mysterious and pugnacious stranger with whose stunning blow my temples yet tingled. Neither he nor my father, however, were visible. Sometimes forms floated before my sight and a silvery murmur of tongues was in my ear, but I saw nothing distinctly.

'Keep off, children,' said my aunt. 'You oppress him with your inquisitiveness. Cecillia, hand me the salts again.'

A fresh application of this restorative brought back my senses. I rose and looked first on one side, then on the other. I had been placed on a sofa near the fire. Earl Seymour sat opposite in an armchair, his foot (I suppose he had the gout) laid on a cushioned stool, and little Helen rubbing it gently with her hands. My other cousins, five in number, all young ladies varying in their ages from twenty to twelve, were crowded round the sofa. They were putting twenty questions to their mother in the same breath.

'Mama, what can be the matter? Has he displeased Augustus? Who was that with our uncle? Why did he keep his face covered, Mama? Why was he so silent? Don't you think he's a strange man?' etc., etc.

'Hush, hush, ugh!' coughed the Earl, their father. 'Be silent, girls, and don't stun one with your larums![8] I say, Isabella, order the whole crew off to bed. I permitted them to stay up so late that they might hear about the funeral, but I suppose you've nothing particular to tell. I must say it's unaccountable in that Duke of Zamorna to do everything so privately. How many mourners were there, pray?'

She was going to answer, when the door opened and Lord Fitzroy entered.

'Well, Mother,' said he, coming swaggering up to the fire, 'I understand there's been bloodshed at this wonderfully select burial. You've come back with a wounded man, eh? There were so few of you that you should have been unanimous. What does Zamorna mean by excluding his relatives in this fashion? Cousins should follow cousins to the grave. Now, for my part, I never so much as saw this Lord Almeida except once about four months since, when he was but nine weeks old, and therefore can't be expected to break my heart for the matter of his death. But then, you see, etiquette compels one to keep house on the night when one's second cousin takes a ride in the cold-meat cart[9], and so one might as well be trotting by the side of the vehicle to see that all's right – were it only for decency's sake.'

'For shame, Brother,' said all his sisters in a breath.

'For shame! Why now, you, Cecillia and Eliza and Georgiana confess, haven't you been grumbling in your own hearts that you couldn't go to Lord Richton's grand concert this evening, where the lights are glaring just opposite and if a window's flung open the music sounds quite distinctly? I'm sure you did. As for Catharine and Agnes and Helen, it's another matter: they'd have to stay at home at all events.'

'My dear Fitzroy,' said Lady Seymour, 'you take the affair very much to heart. I assure you there's no such pleasure in attending a funeral at any time, but especially on so dreary a night as the present.'

'Perhaps not, Mother, but it would be better than cowering in one's own inglenook, listening to the wind blowing a hornpipe in the chimney and you not permitted to dance to it.'

'Fitzroy,' said Lady Cecillia, by way of changing the conversation, 'we've had one of the mourners here. He came with Mama and my uncle, but only stayed five minutes and never spoke a word.'

'Indeed! What was he like?'

'Like the assassin in Uwins' picture[10] in the crimson drawing room, for he had his face covered with a cloak.'

'Humph! Mother, you, of course, know who he was?'

'Indeed I do not. I have never seen him except muffled, as he appeared this evening. But now, children, once for all let me tell you not to trouble me with questions regarding that stranger. I shall answer none you may put to me. Come, loves, it is past one. Bid your father and me goodnight. You should all have been in your chambers long since.'

The girls shook hands with and kissed their parents in succession. Fitzroy more carelessly nodded his head with an awkward air, for I believe the ceremony of bidding goodnight in any shape was unusual to him, and left the room whistling.

In an hour's time the whole mansion from hall to attic was buried in the silence of profound sleep.

CHAPTER THREE

Letter from the Duchess of Zamorna
To Lady Helen Percy

Dear Grandmama,

I have always been accustomed to make you my confidante, to tell you everything, to ask your advice on all subjects. I think my disposition is not very frank – at least, its frankness is not extended. The circle of my bosom friends I like to be small, select, strictly exclusive. My father, the Duke of Wellington, and yourself form the sphere of my concentrated strong affections. It is not in the nature of Northangerland's daughter to be very diffusive in her attachments. There are many others whom I like, many whom I admire, thousands with whom I am on good and cheerful terms, two after whom I have hankerings of natural regard (*id est* my brothers, Edward and William), but the example of my great father has prevented me from wasting among miscellaneous commonplace 'connections' the esteem and tenderness which I owe only to a few. So much for affection. As for love, every drop I possess of that passion is poured out on one grand object: Zamorna has it all, and I could not, if I would, deduct one atom from his right. I wish – oh, how I wish – that he could be sensible of this; that he knew how much, how deeply and how fervently I love him. Then, perhaps, he would not be so sad as he sometimes is – so cold, so strange, so silent.

Grandmama, I have now been married to the Duke half a year. It was a strange thing for me to become the wife of Zamorna! I had dreamt about him years before, seen him through the haze of his glorious poetry, conversed with him in thought, wandered with him in idea through all the scenes his works describe. For hours I have sat under the elm trees of Percy Hall, buried in reveries whose continually recurring theme was that youthful prince and poet. He was a wild dream and superhuman vision, a rainbow apparition which I chased and chased over hill and plain and valley, ever unwearied, never successful, wholly absorbed in the vain yet delicious pursuit. When I at length saw him, when I heard him speak, when I even felt the thrilling touch of his hand, no tongue can express the emotions that almost paralysed me with their power.

In no single thing was he like the being I had imagined to myself, and yet, as on entering the room, I saw a figure rise up as tall as Milton's Satan, as bright as his Ithuriel[11], it needed not speech to furnish me with the name of that figure. My previous ideas had been all indeed sparkling, but vague and indefinite to the last degree. I had imagined him only in romantic situations. I had thought of him only as the inspired boy-minstrel, the life-giving form in a grand landscape where stream and tree and sky and mountain, all flinging their shadows and rolling their waves, bewildered the eye with profusion of magnificence, till it carried away no distinct image of what it had rested upon.

I cannot describe how the reality affected me! It was so new, so fascinating, to behold my hero, my royal lyrist, mingling in the everyday scenes of genuine life. It did not lower him; it flung him out in a new light, a fresh and striking position. Everything he did, everything he said, however trivial, possessed enchaining interest in my eyes. I actually remember watching him with intense solicitude one day, as he was ransacking the Countess of Northangerland's desk for some papers. He flung the manuscripts out in heaps, opened the letters unscrupulously, glanced them rapidly over, laughed at some and sneered at others, tossed the seals and wax and wafers about. Then, being unable to discover the object of his search, he treated her portfolio in the same manner: opened it on the carpet, kneeling on one knee, squandered the contents about most recklessly, looking all the while so eager, his eyes lighted and face a little flushed. There were several persons in the room, the Countess herself among the number. She regarded him very complacently and never offered to stop his proceedings. Even when he asked for the key of her cabinet, she gave it him and let him commit the same ravages there.

The first time I saw him eat, too, was an era in my life. It was one teatime at Ellrington Hall. I presided at table and he sat next me on a music stool, which sort of sofa he always prefers at that meal. I was so absorbed in listening to and watching him that I quite forgot to enquire whether he took tea or coffee, etc., but handed him the cup nearest my hand. It stood before him a minute without being touched.

He then said with a smile, 'Do you know, Miss Percy, you have given me a vessel of liquid which I can't taste: milk, sugar and green tea – an intolerable compound.' So saying, he emptied it into the slop-basin and requested a cup of unmixed mocha coffee.

As I hurriedly complied, he whispered to me in his own low, sweet tone: 'Be perfect in your business, Mary, before the time comes when I may be your only guest, seated opposite in a snug drawing room with Roland and Roswal couched amiably on the rug.'

These words made my heart throb almost audibly. I little thought then how near they were to fulfilment. The block of his existing marriage shut out any ideas of the kind, indeed that very evening the Marchioness was present. She sat at my left hand and her eyes were never off her lord. To no one else would I mention the name of that lady. I shudder whenever I think of her, not with hatred – I believe, Grandmama, it is not in my nature to hate such a one as she was; nay, I should have loved her had she been the wife of anyone else – but with horror at her ghastly fate. Were that fate to be *mine*, were Zamorna to leave me and marry another, I should die, not of consumption, but of a sudden paroxysm of life-quenching agony that would cut me down like a scythe. Good God, at times I have had glimpses of the anguish she endured so patiently. I have had sudden pangs of jealousy and moments of unutterable darkness, and while they lasted my spirit boiled in lava. I had feelings of suffocation and terrific goading sensations that almost drove me mad. And then when the creature whom I suspected to be my rival was present, I turned sheet-white with abhorrence. And when I could find Zamorna alone, I begged him to kill me at once, and kneeled before him, and bathed his hand in tears that he himself said were scalding. He always heard me; he always pitied me; but he said I was foolish and mistaken, and tried to cheer me with his wild musical laugh, and never in vain, for that laugh, when not fierce or scornful, is a cordial itself to my ears.

But, Grandmama, my pen has run away from me. I have written on anything rather than the subject I intended to, which is certain inconsistencies in the Duke's conduct that at times puzzle me most painfully. Since our marriage it has been my constant study, the business of my life, to watch the unfolding of his strange character, to read his heart (if I could), to become acquainted with all his antipathies that I might avoid them, and all his inclinations that I might continually follow them. Sometimes my efforts have been successful, sometimes unsuccessful, but upon the whole my attention or *tact* – as the Duke of Wellington calls it – has rather raised than lowered me in his good opinion. You know I am practised in this kind of silent vigilance. I used to exercise it towards my dear father. Ever since I can remember I have watched the proper moments when to speak and when to be silent. I have studied his likes and dislikes, and rigidly striven to gratify the former and avoid the latter. It was natural for me then, when I became the wife of one whom I loved so inexpressibly as Zamorna, to exert every effort in order to please him. Yet in spite of all, sometimes he is unaccountably cool – not unkind, I cannot say that – but it is the kindness of a friend rather than a husband. And then he changes so suddenly. And there are other little mysterious incidents connected with these changes which nobody saw but me and which I reveal to none. An example or two will best explain my meaning.

About a week ago he came into my room one morning in travelling equipment and said he was going to Angria. He bade me goodbye very tenderly, and I felt as if I had never loved him till then. I gazed in the direction his carriage had gone long after it was invisible, and the whole day was fit for little except moping with my head on my hand. Evening came. I was too fretful to enjoy company, so instead of attending any of the numerous parties to which I was engaged, I stayed at home sitting by the fire of the small library with splendour and comfort around and insuperable wretchedness within. I think it was about ten o'clock and my low spirits were at their depth when the door opened, and the Duke of Zamorna walked in. Astonishment and delight kept me fixed to my seat a minute. He came forward, laid his hand on the back of a chair, and looked full at me but did not speak. I was presently at his side, and my arms were clasped round his neck. He attempted to loose them, but so faintly and smiling at the same time that I thought he was only in play. Just then a fierce growl, almost like that of a large dog, startled me. The Duke directly shook off my hold. He held me at arm's length, and, still smiling, looked through my eyes into my very heart.

'Dear Arthur,' said I, 'what happy turn in the wheel of fortune has brought you back so soon?'

'I don't know whether it is happy or not, Mary,' said he. 'You appear so much surprised to see me.'

I made no answer. There was something very singular in the expression with which he regarded me. And at that moment the apparition of Finic glided in between us, and, gently yet firmly removing me from the Duke's touch, began to converse with him by means of signs. I looked on in silence as they wove their fingers into words as quickly as lightning, my lord, every now and then, fixing his speaking eyes on the mute's countenance and reading what he would say there faster than even the language of signs could inform him.

'What is all this coming to?' I asked myself. The Duke soon spoke.

'Mary,' said he, 'I ought to be at Angria. Therefore you will say nothing of this unlooked-for return. I shall remain but five minutes. My purpose in entering this apartment was merely to write a letter.'

Materials stood on the table. He sat down and hastily wrote, folded and sealed a small billet. I noticed that he did not use his royal signet ring, which indeed was absent from his finger, but a small seal ring on his left hand, engraved with the arms of Wellesley not Angria. He rose when he had finished, took his travelling cap, which, as he placed it rather forward, threw, in conjunction with the curls that the rim pressed down, a deep shadow over his brow and eyes. He then surveyed me all over with a quick stolen, keenly penetrating glance and, uttering a careless 'goodnight', was about to leave the room. I started towards him, hardly knowing what I was about.

'Dear Arthur,' said I, 'won't you shake hands with me before you go?'

He laughed and turned his face from me to Finic. The creature stamped and gesticulated impatiently as if he wished him to depart.

'Is that dwarf to control your motions, my lord?' said I. 'I wish he were at the bottom of the night!'

'And so do I, too,' was the reply. 'He is a decided bore – yet a useful one. But come, give me your hand and never mind his ill temper.'

My hand had scarcely touched his when Finic set up a perfect yell. He jumped, contorted his hideous features, writhed as if a knife had been stuck into him, and in short exhibited every symptom of ludicrous and malignant rage. He need not have been in such alarm: I hardly felt the pressure of Zamorna's fingers, it was so slight and cold. His Grace seemed highly amused; he laughed heartily both at me and the dwarf. I thought he appeared inclined to prolong the entertainment, for he shut the door, which stood open, and once or twice approached where I stood, but then Finic began to look dangerous and to roll his white eyes most savagely.

'Hah!' said Zamorna. 'It's time to be gone, that's evident.' He hastily bid me 'goodnight', fetched Finic a tremendous blow with the butt-end of a pistol which he drew from his breast, saying, 'Take that, dog, for your causeless clamour,' and strode out of the apartment.

Now, Grandmama, what do you think of all this? Is it not passing strange? And this is not the only scene of the kind I have been an actor in. Twice or thrice has the same scene been played over before. I cannot conceive what earthly right that dwarf has to intervene between me and my lord, much less how his haughty spirit can submit to it. Then the origin of his fits of coldness and caution I shall never be able to ascertain. They are only fits, for sometimes he is far otherwise than cold, but that makes the intervals more insufferable. Then again, generally speaking, Finic hardly dares lift his eyes in his presence, he is abject and crawling as an earthworm. I verily believe Oedipus only could solve the whole enigma.[12]

I have written myself into a very moody humour, and it is past twelve at night, so, dear Grandmama, farewell,

Your affectionate granddaughter,
Mary Henrietta Wellesley

PS It is a common saying that the postscript of a woman's letter always contains the pith and marrow of what she intended to write, the matter nearest her heart. I believe my present communication will offer no exception to this general rule. Doubtless you have heard of the Marquis Almeida's death. I never knew it till the newspapers formally announced the fact to the public. The name of that young prince has not once dropped from Zamorna's lips in my hearing. From the first moment of our acquaintance till now he is delicately reserved in all relating to former connections, though I fear they dwell on his mind. Well, my stepson was buried a fortnight ago at midnight, in the royal vault of Wellesley. I understand the occupants of Grassmere together with two strangers, with whom nobody is acquainted, were present at the funeral.

Grandmama, I would just now give a thousand pounds to know who Ernest Fitz-Arthur is. Undeniably Zamorna is his father, of that I am satisfied, for I have seen the child, but who claims the honour of being his mother? I know whom you would mention, but your guess is wrong, not M.L. I solemnly asked Edward, and he as solemnly and most promptly replied in the negative. This assurance put me on my mettle. It roused all the latent sparks of female curiosity which are contained in my nature, and those are neither few nor feeble. I determined to know if I could, and I think I have been at least partially successful. Having learnt from Charles that Ernest and his guardian were still residing at Douro Villa, it came into my head, one fine evening last week, that I would take a ride over and visit them. I longed to see whether Miss Laury was so handsome, and Fitz-Arthur so much like his father as people said. It was hazardous, for I incurred the risk of my lord's displeasure if he should find me out, but curiosity – curiosity, that oversteps most obstacles with women – and as the Duke was then at Adrianopolis, two hundred miles off, I hoped there was no great danger. Well, I ordered the carriage and set out.

It was just two hours before sunset as I entered the grounds, and a serenely solemn evening that brought Percy Hall to my remembrance. I alighted before coming in sight of the villa as I did not wish the sound of wheels to give notice of my approach. Turning aside from the main path, I took a shorter one which wound among the trees close by the terrace ground where the gardens are planted. All seemed so silent, so calm, and shady, and peaceful in the upper region that I could not resist the temptation of ascending its grassy slope and walking for a little while in those deep, dim alleys that opened like glimpses of Paradise far within. I wandered on, lost in thought, till, at a sudden turn, the splash of a fountain fell on my ear, and I thought a low murmur of tongues mingled with the fall of waters. Softly I stole forward. Trees grew round, and, without being myself seen, I could observe the spirits haunting these solemn groves. A Narcissus of Chantrey's[13], carved in marble, was bending over the basin of the spring.

Close beside, flesh and blood exquisitely in contrast with lifeless stone, sat a lady and *two* children. Yes, Grandmama, two! When I saw that, I was really startled.

The lady I instantly recognised as Mina Laury. Her tall form, black eyes and hair, and clear brunette complexion were sufficient landmarks to go by. Handsome she certainly is and that I do not wonder at (many of our peasantry are so), but her perfect elegance is more astonishing. She might be an earl's instead of a cottager's daughter. I trembled when I saw her, but I trembled still more when I saw the cherub-like children – a boy and girl, one four, the other perhaps two years old, so exquisitely beautiful, so full of life, their glancing curls and brilliant smiling eyes throwing into such death-like stillness the carved figure with its cold gleaming limbs and sightless orbs behind them. And then the likeness – aye, that was the bitter, the stinging ingredient that poisoned the whole lovely spectacle. I wish their eyes had been blue; I wish their hair had been flaxen; then I could have loved them but, as it was, when I saw my own husband's features in fine miniature, when I beheld myself gazed at by his very eyes – the same remarkable, dark, transparent, sepia brown, with unvariegated iris of a clear even tint, and large full pupils – their beauty sickened me. The little girl was the very counterpart of her brother, only her skin was even more delicately fair, and, mingled with the likeness of Zamorna, there was a slight alien touch that turned her features into a more feminine mould. They were lying on the edge of the fountain, floating leaves and flowers on its surface, and watching them as the whirl of the falling stream caught and sucked them into its vortex. Mina kept guard that no danger might ensue. Oh, it was a fair scene, as the mingling light and shadows of the grove fell on the whole reposing group – if I could have enjoyed it, but I could not.

Scarcely conscious what I did, I came forward, and sat down opposite Mina.

'You seem fond of children, Miss Laury,' I said.

At the sound of my voice she raised her head calmly, her countenance betrayed no surprise. Steadily surveying me she answered, 'Of my master's, I am, madam.'

'Aye, and of your master's self, too, I have no doubt,' said I, with – I believe – my father's sneer, for my heart was choking in my throat.

'Ladies equal to himself in birth and connections may say they are fond of the Duke of Zamorna,' she replied, 'but that is not the word I should use.'

'And pray what word would you use?'

'He is my master, madam, therefore I honour him.'

I laughed scornfully for my blood was up.

'You are a hypocrite, Miss Laury,' said I, 'you do more than honour him.'

'Yes, I worship and obey him.'

'And is that all?'

'I love him.'

'Anything more.'

'I would die for him.'

'You would not!' said I. 'I could not do more and I am confident there is not a woman on earth would do as much for him as I myself.'

'Delicate, soft-bred, brittle creature,' returned she, with kindling eyes, 'that is an empty boast! The spirit might carry you far, but the body would break down at last. My lady Duchess – for I know you by the Percy forehead and golden hair – it is not for an indulged daughter of aristocracy, for one who from her birth has hardly ever breathed out of the perfumed atmosphere of palace halls, or trod elsewhere than on velvet soft carpets, to talk of serving Zamorna. She may please and entertain him and blossom brightly in his smiles, but when adversity saddens him, when there are hard duties to perform, when his brow grows dark and his voice becomes stern and sounds only in command, I warn you, he will call for another handmaid, one whose foot is as familiar to wild and common as to gilded saloon, who knows the feel of a hard bed and the taste of a dry crust, who has been rudely nurtured and not shielded like a hothouse flower from every blast of chilling wind. And besides, my lady, Zamorna's work wants a heart and a mind different from yours, beautiful patrician. With what morbid delicacy would you shrink from scenes that I have looked on unmoved? How the exotic's leaves would fold and bow down as the shadows of sorrow and death fell like night on their loveliness. The noble and high born cannot endure grief. They fly with cowardly terror from the coming of mortality, and when it grasps them or theirs, what wild, impious wailings fill dome and turret, bower and hall. It is not so in cottages. Poverty and the necessity of labour strengthen men's souls wonderfully.' She paused. For a minute I was much too astonished to reply. This was not the kind of language I expected from her and at first it threw me off my guard. Northangerland's daughter, however, was not long to be baffled.

'Miss Laury,' said I, 'what right have you to rank me with the frail painted trinkets you have described? I acknowledge myself to be of noble blood, and I glory in my descent, for never – either in past or present times – has a son or daughter of the house of Percy shrunk from danger, or trembled before affliction. I know who you have in mind, girl. I will be candid. At this moment your thoughts rest on your late mistress.'

'They do,' said she. Then, solemnly bending her large dark eyes on my face, continued. 'She was as sweet and mild and fair as you, my lady. She was as earnest as you seem to be in her devotion to the Duke. She, too, used to talk about her strength of mind and powers of endurance. But how silently, how rapidly, she faded when her hour came! There was no impulse in her heart which prompted her to live for him after he ceased to live for her, nor is there in yours. But listen, I hear a step. Now comes a being of the same order as yourself. Talk to her, I am too humble for such conference.'

As a sound of footsteps approached, the flashing, lighted expression which filled Mina's countenance died away, her eyes fell, and a shadow of quiet melancholy, which I believe habitual to her, settled on her brow. Meanwhile a lady appeared advancing down the alley. She was richly dressed and her mien was stately; two others, seemingly attendants, followed behind. As she drew near I retired a little backwards, as I wished to make my observations unperceived. She was young, perhaps about nineteen, but of a rather tall figure; her motions and port displayed an almost queenly assumption of dignity, yet her features had a soft and graceful rather than a majestic character. She resembled the most beautiful portraits I have seen of Mary Stuart[14] in her best days: the same fascinating turn of countenance, the same animated eyes, white neck and winning mouth. Her hair was dark glossy brown; it fell in thick ringlets over her neck and temples but did not rest on her shoulders. Her polished taper-fingers were sparkling with rings, and round her neck there was a rosary of foam-white pearls, having a gold cross at the end like the one Jordan gave me when I was a little girl. This was a delightful spectacle for me, Grandmama, was it not? However, I looked and was silent.

'Well, Mina,' said she, 'watching your charges, I perceive, as usual. You are a good girl, a valuable girl. My little Emily already appears to like you as well as Ernest, and neither of them, I fear, will be able to part with you when it is necessary. What say you, Edward?'

'I like Mina,' replied the boy, 'and I always call her mama when you are away, but Papa says boys should never think it impossible to do without a woman or to part with her, so when I go back to Castle Oronsay I'll always remember Mina, but be sure, Mother, I'll not cry about her.'

'But I will,' said his sister with a soft infantine lisp. 'And Mina must go back with us. Mama, tell Papa to make her.'

'My darling,' said the lady, caressing her little dark-eyed Emily. 'I wish I could gratify you. Miss Laury, do you think it utterly impossible to accompany us?'

'I am at my master's disposal, madam,' replied Miss Laury. 'His determination must be mine.'

'Surely he will not send you back to the manor house now,' continued her interrogator, 'without either Ernest or Julius you would die of loneliness.'

'Scarcely that,' returned Mina with a smile, 'for there would be Mrs Lancaster, and Mr Sumner, who remains at Keswick, though he will no longer be an inmate at Grassmere, besides the people at the lodge, Lady Millicent Hume, and Euphemia Lindsay with the old dame.'

'You are quite willing to be mistress of the haunted chateau again then?'

'Yes, if the Duke commanded it. But he has hinted that Mornington Court will be my next destination. Grassmere manor house is to be shut up and consigned to the care of the steward and his wife.'

'Well,' said the lady, 'I, of course, dare not interfere with

Zamorna's movements, yet I wish he would allow my children the advantage of your superintendence a little longer. My maidens here, Blanche and Harriet, are good girls, but something of the giddiest when compared with you. Well, well, it is my fault, I spoil them.'

Just then her eye fell on me for I had again drawn near.

'Hah!' said she. 'Who is that? A fair creature, by Our Lady. Don't you think, Harriet,' turning to her attendant, 'she would make a sweeter Madonna than even that celestial image in my oratory?'

'Aye, madam,' was the reply, 'but what would my lord say to such Madonnas? Would he not worship them himself, think you? And, however much you might wish for his conversion, would you employ such means to obtain it?'

She shook her head and was grave a minute, but soon returned to her former gay mood.

'Tell me your name, pretty one,' said she, looking on me with an aspect of condescension.

I made no answer, but I felt myself tremble and turn pale with passion. So long as she abstained from addressing herself directly to me I could bear it, but when, with an air of proud affability such as a queen might use to a rosy-cheeked peasant girl, she dared to ask my name and bestow on me a half-contemptuous half-endearing epithet, I felt all the Percy rise in my soul. I believe she thought me a mere child. I had on only a plain satin frock and beaver hat, and you, Grandmama, always say I look very young in that dress, not more than fifteen or sixteen perhaps. Seeing me change colour she continued, 'You are not ill I hope, my dear? Why, gracious! Harriet, see how like marble her face looks, as pale and shining as that Narcissus bending over the fountain. Blanche, be quick, sprinkle a little water on her, or she will faint.'

'Madam, madam,' whispered Miss Laury, in a hurried yet deferential tone, 'be on your guard, that is the Duchess of Zamorna.'

'The Duchess of Zamorna!' echoed the lady, in a voice of strong surprise. 'Impossible! So young a creature! Why, Augustus – but I need not say anything; *I* was married at fifteen.'

I advanced and said, I suppose in a more energetic manner than she expected, for she stepped back and crossed herself two or three times, 'Madam, whoever you are, don't dare to say you are married, I deny it, and were Zamorna himself to swear you were his wife I would not believe him. You, Zamorna's wife? What then, that boy is his heir, for I suppose you will not disown him as your son.'

'Never!' said she, drawing Ernest towards her. 'He is indeed my son, my first born and most cherished son. Whether he is Zamorna's heir or not, time will show.'

'You need not equivocate,' said I, 'for I will not bear it. Do you think Alexander Percy's daughter will tamely suffer her rights to be appropriated by pretenders? No, be undeceived if such are your opinions! Woman, I hate you!'

This was said in the full sincerity of my soul. It made her tell the pearls on her rosary, but to my astonishment roused no feeling of anger, at least, no *apparent* feeling.

'I am sensible,' she returned, 'that your case appears very hard, and at present I can offer no explanation, my lips are indissolubly sealed.'

'Don't cant,' said I. 'Don't extenuate. It will admit of no explanation. Are those children Zamorna's or are they not?'

She frowned, blushed, ran her fingers from one end to the other of her beads, and was silent.

'Hah!' said I. 'You cannot say no, the mark is on them,

indisputable, ineffaceable. Look at those eyes!' And, between passion and grief, I burst into tears.

The lady passed her hand across her brow with a gesture of weariness; she heaved a deep sigh and sat down. Ernest now addressed me.

'Leave off crying,' said he. 'I pity you very much. But why do you speak so angrily to Mama? You make her sad. Papa would frown if he heard you; he never lets anybody say a quick word to her. She is a great lady, and would love you if you were not so cross.'

'Yes,' said little Emily, 'as much as she loves me, and you might visit her perhaps at Castle Oronsay. Papa, if you asked him, would bring you in his carriage when he comes.'

'To be sure he would,' resumed Ernest. 'Emily is quite right. But take notice, my lady, if you were a man and had spoken so to Mama, I should hate you and you might never come to Castle Oronsay then, for the Duke, my father' – he spoke these words proudly – 'would stab you to the heart before you should enter his gates.'

These words only made me cry more. Tears now began to steal down the cheek of the lady, tears of happiness I imagine, for she had her noble boy to plead for her. At this crisis, a dark shade fell suddenly on the waters of the fountain. As I stood with my face to it and my back to the entrance of the grove, it seemed to mingle with my reflected figure and far to overtop it. I knew there was something behind me, but what? My blood froze and my flesh quivered as accents, whose music was too familiar, murmured the reply in my ear. 'Mary, you are out late tonight; the sun has set a quarter of an hour. In God's name, go home.'

A dash amongst the trees followed these warning words; the reflection suddenly vanished. I turned: nothing was visible, only the boughs waved wildly in one part and a shower of roses was descending on the green walk.

'Papa, Papa,' exclaimed Ernest, and plunging amongst the agitated foliage he likewise disappeared, calling down a fresh shower of fluttering leaves from the shaken branches. I dared not follow. Nothing remained for me but instant obedience, so, bowing low, more in pride than courtesy to my still weeping rival, I returned to the carriage, which I found waiting, entered it and drove off. Here I must pause for the present. My postscript has run on nearly to twice the length of my letter.

Farewell, dear Grandmama, no vicissitudes, no trials can make me forget you. Answer me quickly, and believe, etc., etc.

M.H. Wellesley

CHAPTER FOUR

Dear Grandmama,

I will now take up the thread of my narrative where I dropped it and proceed in regular order. On reaching Wellesley House after my stolen visit to Douro Villa, I retired instantly to my apartment. The chaotic confusion of fears, hopes and conjectures which filled my mind rendered me wholly unfit for society of any kind. Who was that lady? Was she really the wife of Zamorna, as she had as good as affirmed? Why had the Duke departed so hastily after speaking to me? Was he angry with me? How did it come to pass that, instead of being at Angria, he was in the Valley of Verdopolis? And was there any likelihood of his returning to the city that night? Could I in that case summon courage to ask for an explanation? Would he give it me? Such were the questions I asked and re-asked myself, always in vain. None stood near to give me an answer. I sighed and wept and almost wished that Zamorna had ever remained a dream to me, and that the reality had never dawned in such bright but troubling glory.

There was one thing which seemed beyond a doubt, and that was the relationship of the Duke to those two children. Every look, tone and gesture of the boy, young as he was, asserted the fact and confirmed it with indisputable testimony. While I was pondering on these things, a low sigh, as from someone close at hand, broke the train of my sad reflections. I glanced hurriedly round, almost expecting to see the Duke, though his appearance is not commonly heralded by a sigh. The chamber was filled with moonlight, streaming through the large Venetian windows over which the curtains were not yet dropped. Nothing appeared darkening that faint lustre, and I should have lapsed again into meditation had not a hand touched mine as it rested on the little flower stand near which I sat.

Good God! My heart sprang to my throat, for at that instant the ghastly, deformed figure of Finic glided into the light, and, with a shuddering moan, sank in a heap before me. Forgetting that he could neither hear nor answer, I asked, gently as I could, what he wanted. I cannot say that I was afraid of the creature, for he always treats me with profound respect, bowing lower than an eastern slave whenever he enters my presence, and I in return have shielded him from some annoyances arising from the antipathy of the servants to his unsightly exterior. Yet, in spite of the good understanding which this reciprocation of kind offices has established between us, and which has only been broken by the odd system of interference mentioned in my last letter, I must confess I felt strongly inclined to ring the bell and summon a few witnesses to behold our conference. As I was rising for this purpose, he lifted his huge head, and, flinging back his matted locks so that the moonbeams had full leave to pour their revealing radiance on each wild and exaggerated feature of his unearthly visage, he fixed his eyes on mine with an expression of pathos and entreaty which I could not resist. It was the more moving because in his general moods he is sullen, ferocious, misanthropic and malignant – so, at least, the servants say, though with me he is usually gentle enough. I sat down and, patting his shaggy head in order to soothe the morbid gloom of his temperament, I again asked what he wanted, but this time it was by signs, not speech. I can converse with him pretty readily in that way, but then it's by the ordinary and well-known method, not those occult movements with which he and Zamorna hold communion in a matter intelligible only to themselves, and whose lightning rapidity so dazzles the eyes of spectators that it would be vain to attempt learning it through the medium of observation.

The following conversation ensued in terms as concise as a telegraphic dispatch.

FINIC (in answer to my first question): You have done wrong.

MYSELF: In what?

FINIC: In your day's visit.

MYSELF: What follows?

FINIC: Danger.

MYSELF: Of the Duke's anger?

FINIC: Of the Duke's death.

MYSELF (after a pause, for this reply stunned me at first): What do you mean?

FINIC: What I say! The act has been so near committed that a portion, at least, if not the whole, of the penalty will be exacted.

MYSELF: I do not understand you.

FINIC: Perhaps not, but so it is. You should not have been jealous. You should not have given way to curiosity. So long as Zamorna's love was yours, what mattered if it was not wholly yours?

'Then,' I exclaimed aloud, 'it is true, she is his wife!'

He did not hear this, and, recollecting myself, I put the question in a manner he could comprehend.

'Most true,' was the reply, 'the Lady of Oronsay is the Duke's wife.'

I could proceed no further; my brain whirled, my heart died within me. How long I remained in a state of torpor – torpor to everything but a sensation of the most exquisite agony –

I know not. But when I did at length arouse to something like remembrance, I looked round for Finic and saw that he was gone. A thousand questions immediately rushed on me which I wished to have asked him. I knew it would be vain to call him back, as he never resumes a subject after he has once dismissed it.

That night sleep and I were strangers. The whole of the next day I continued in a state which you, my dear Grandmama, may imagine, but which I cannot describe. Haunted by the shadow of that danger to my lord so vaguely hinted at, and by the still darker shadow of his apprehended displeasure, cursing my foolish jealousy while the flame of that very jealousy was kindling every moment still fiercer in my bosom, watching, praying for his return, yet dreading it as the herald of fresh afflictions, night came and went. The next day, and the next, and the next glided away, or rather crept as if loaded with lead. I heard no word, no syllable of him, yet dispatches arrived regularly from Adrianopolis to his secretaries here, and they were all sealed with his seal and signed with his autograph. He could not, therefore, be *now* at Douro Villa. There was some consolation in that reflection.

At last, on the evening of the fifth day, he came. I was in the drawing room surrounded with a throng of company when he entered accompanied by my brother. Edward looked vigorous and bright, and was evidently in the highest spirits, but alas, I saw that Zamorna was wasted, weary and wan. The curse, then, had fallen on him, and I was the cause.

So many pressed round him on his entrance that it was long before I, conscience-stricken as I was, could come near enough to address him. While I stood apart I saw Maria, my sister-in-law, go fearlessly forward to welcome *her* husband, and Edward smiled on her so kindly and grasped her hand so warmly that I nearly burst into tears at the thought of the contrast my reception was likely to afford.

'Zamorna,' I heard Mr Montmorency say, 'what on earth ails you? You have been working too hard, man! Upon my word, this won't do! If you stand labour no better than this, we may as well turn you over to the undertaker at once.'

'Why, Mont,' replied my husband easily, 'I say, what on earth ails you? Surely you see through a jaundiced medium. It is you who need the kindness of the undertaker. As for me, the bell of St Michael's now tolling is rottenness itself when compared with the soundness of my mental and corporeal condition.'

'A mere brag!' said Montmorency, taking a large pinch of snuff. 'Mr Edward, what do you say?'

'I say he lies!' replied my brother in his decided way. 'And for the last day or two, I promise you, this same Duke of Zamorna has been forced to hear a piece of my mind respecting his want of appetite, paring of flesh – as the rare apes say – desperately moody humours and the like absurd trash. If he does not alter, I'll wrest the sceptre out of his hand and clap a distaff[15] in its place.'

'Oh Hector!'[16] said the Duke in the same gay tone, unbonneting in the meantime and displaying his eyes and curls as beautiful as ever, and the former flashing with even unwonted brilliancy. 'Oh Hector, who shall put a bridle in thy mouth and a bit on thy tongue? Brother, do you see you have chased the roses from more than one fair cheek. By my honour, ladies, I am proud of your sympathy, but sweet as it is, you may spare it. Zamorna will not die yet, though all the owls on earth should croak his doom and scream his epitaph. I'll live, by heaven, to spite *them*, to spite *him*!'

This was said in a voice of firm emphasis, and with a glance of defiance directed, not at any particular person, but at something seen rather with the mind's eye than with the bodily organs.

What could he mean? The momentary excitement passed away, and he stood as calm and cheerful as before.

Now I drew nigh. I would have spoken, I would have said something about my sorrow for his altered appearance, but the words died on my lips. I could only put my hand into his.

'Well, Mary,' said he, 'do *you* think me a walking skeleton, a sort of living symbol of death, as it were, a creature lingering on the surface of the earth when it ought to be asleep in her centre?' These words showed me that there was a morbid feeling about him, a feverish sensibility which exaggerated every idea that it caught. I only answered, '*Dear* Arthur, I am glad to see you!'

'What!' he said. 'Glad to see me dying?' And turned away with an ironical laugh.

Heavily did the remainder of that party pass. Though the Duke himself was even wildly gay, yet he could not communicate a corresponding spirit to his guests. They saw it was all assumed and hollow-hearted, and all that sort of cheerfulness is more depressing to a spectator than the most determined melancholy. At length they began to depart. Group after group left the rooms, carriage after carriage rolled from the door, the full flood of 'rings and plumes and pearls'[17], which had inundated every apartment, ebbed away till only a few scanty streamlets remained. These sunk dry also, and, as the timepiece chimed four, and I made my last bow to my last retiring guest, the door closed and we were alone. *We*, that is, I and my lord. With a beating heart I turned towards him. Now was my time of trial, now I was to learn whether or not his anger lay heavy on me, whether, too, he could bear up against sickness as well in solitude as he had done in society. Alas, the last question was soon decided.

I saw him flung into a chair, his head hanging back in an attitude of deathly languor, his eyes closed, and his hands pressed to his forehead. The breezes of dawn were now shaking the saloon windows, and its cold light streamed through those that looked to the east, mingling in sickly unison with the pale, faded gleam of unextinguished sconce and chandelier. By this lustre I beheld my husband. It added an alien melancholy to what was already too deeply distressing in itself. I went and stood beside him. He neither looked at nor spoke to me. My heart nearly wept blood to see his eyes so quenched, his brow so darkened, his cheek and lips so marble pale, all his glory in fact bowed in the dust of mortality. Unconsciously I bent over him; my breath stirred his hair; he opened his eyes.

'Ah, Mary,' said he, while a faint smile lit his exhausted features, 'you see I'm but in a poor way. It's vain to deny it any longer. I've struggled against the blight while I could, but now the flesh yields, though the spirit would still defy him. Sit down, love, you will not understand my wild language. I fear I shall rave terribly if delirium comes over me.'

I sat down, glad of any support which could keep me from dropping on the floor. I felt exceedingly faint and my joints shook like aspen leaves. His kindness I now felt was worse to bear than his sternest anger could have been. Remorse was now my portion and I felt it to be unutterably bitter. He drew me to his side and, resting his forehead on my shoulder, said, 'Mary, you have heard of no strange report in the city, have you?'

I answered as well as I could, speaking in the negative.

'That is odd,' he returned. 'If the discovery had been made

it would have spread like wildfire. But perhaps it has not, and the abhorred wretch is taking a base advantage of some false start.'

After a momentary pause, he rose up and, pacing the room with long and rapid strides, exclaimed, 'Who has been tampering with my private affairs? Who has been prying into that which I chose to keep a sealed and solemn secret? Whose hand picked the lock? Whose eye gazed on the treasure? By all that's holy, by all that's infernal (for there's less of heaven than hell in the business), if it be a man, I'll have the sacrifice of his life for an atonement; if it be a woman, she's marked henceforth with the brand of Zamorna's eternal hatred.

'Great Genii![18] To die now, to go down in the first burst of existence to a cold and obscure grave, to leave all my glory ungathered, all my hopes spread like a golden harvest, to quit the field which was ripe for the sickle when I had just gone forth with my reapers,[19] to leave my kingdom desolate, my name a byword to one who promised like a god, but fulfilled like a wretched earth-sprung man, to see all this great curse come upon me for some villain's insolent curiosity, it would breathe insane life into the lungs of a corpse and warm the red ice stagnating in its veins to the heat of the boiling flood now rushing through mine! I could swear that the pitiful crime is the work of a woman, some impulse of malignant curiosity. Thus they have always overthrown the greatest fabrics of man's construction! Perhaps there has been jealousy in the matter. Hah!' And he looked at *me*.

At that moment I was actuated only by one feeling and one fervid wish: for the earth to rend under me and suck me into its deepest recesses. I shrunk together beneath his gaze, which though I did not see I felt, as if it had been living fire. A thousand years of happiness could never blot this moment of intense suffering from my memory. I could not speak; my tongue and soul were both withered. A mist spread over my eyes and a melancholy sound moaned in my ears, through which I heard the tinkle of a bell. Shortly after, I was sensible someone entered the room. Then followed a dead silence. Then faint wailings as of a human being in bitter distress. I gradually recovered so far as to discern Finic crouched at the feet of his master, shaking his shaggy head, and, while his hands raised above it answered the signs made by Zamorna, his lips uttered the boding murmurs which had roused my attention. Their conference was not long. As it concluded the Duke approached me. Overwhelmed with terror, not knowing what I did, utterly deprived of my presence of mind, I started up and ran towards the door.

'Mary,' said he, in his deepest voice, 'come back. You surely are not afraid of bodily injury from me?'

I blindly obeyed him, more through instinct than anything else.

'Well,' he said half-playfully, 'you are the criminal, I find. You took into your head to go to Douro Villa, did you, my fair Duchess? Merely to have a look at Mina Laury and young Fitz-Arthur, with whom, by the by madam, you had nothing to do more than you have with the inhabitants of Kamschatka[20]. You saw there one or two whom you did not expect to see. You were warned off the premises by myself, so at least Finic tells me. And in short, by your cursed woman's spirit of in-quisitiveness, you have given my greatest enemy an advantage over me which he is now improving to your heart's content. The pains of death have laid hold on me, madam. I shall pass off ere long, I suppose, and leave *you* at liberty. Don't tremble and turn pale. Here, lean on my arm, as you seem about to faint. I don't hate you, Mary, you could not help your prying weakness; it was born with you, as it is with all your sex. But then, my girl' – and he smiled coldly and tapped my neck with ineffable contempt – 'I despise you thoroughly.'

'Arthur,' said I, gathering strength from the violence of the shock I received, 'your scorn is superfluous. I am already crushed by such a load of misery as never before bowed the head of a mortal woman to the ashes of repentance. I have sinned, but my punishment is disproportioned to my crime.'

'Poor thing,' he replied, taking my hand and regarding me with a look of mingled contempt and compassion. 'Don't accuse yourself too harshly. You have not sinned, nothing of the kind – all wretched feminine imbecility which is now showing itself in another shape. Come, madam, cannot we have a tear or two? That should have been your resource at the first approach of the storm.'

'Adrian, I cannot cry,' said I, 'my tears are all dried up with burning anguish, yet –' I was going on, but just then they rushed at once and unbidden to my eyes. My heart swelled with suffocating sorrow; I sank on my knees and, in a voice choked with sobs, exclaimed, 'Oh Zamorna, do take pity on me! Forgive me this once! If I had known, if I had in the faintest degree imagined that one hair of my husband's noble head could have been injured by what I did, I would rather have cut off my right hand than stirred a step on that cursed journey!'

'I have nothing to forgive you,' he replied. 'Of course, I am well enough aware that you did not mean to harm me, only I cannot help smiling at the whole female character, so finely epitomised in you: weakness, errors, repentance. Go away, child, I can talk to you no longer; this curse is overpowering me. Oh, fiend! Demon! It is your time to triumph now, but I will be victor hereafter! Thrust me down to the tomb! I give you leave, but I'll spring up again, for the marble jaws of that devourer will not open to receive me!' He laid his hand on his heart and shuddered as if some inward pang were at that moment rending his very vitals.

How I felt no words can express. But I suppose some of my utter wretchedness appeared in my countenance for suddenly he clasped me to him, and said, 'My dear Mary, don't look so very unhappy. There now, love, there's a kiss of perfect forgiveness; those sad eyes will *make* me love them. Go to your chamber, Henrietta, and fear nothing for me. I'll wrestle it out alone. Death or victory! These torments cannot last long. I shall soon either be a corpse or convalescent, so cheer up, dearest; forget that I said that I would despise you, and take another kiss to seal the pardon of the last.'

With these words he left me. I went up to my chamber, not to sleep you may be sure, but to brood on my sorrows, to strive in vain to unfold the dark mystery in which the whole affair was involved, and to drink up the bitter cup which remorse held to my lips.

Grandmama, I can write no more at present, so farewell.

I am yours,

M.H. Wellesley

CHAPTER FIVE

Extracts from the Journal of Dr Alford,
Physician in Ordinary to the Duke of Zamorna

1ST JULY

This morning, while I was at breakfast, a servant came in with a note, brought, he said, by one of the Duchess of Zamorna's footmen. It was in Her Grace's own slender jessamine hand, and to the following purport:

> *Dear Doctor,*
> *Come to me as soon as ever you can. I am nearly distracted.*
> *My lord, the hope of so many hearts, is, I fear, in a hopeless*
> *condition. He has been ill three days, but would not permit*
> *me to call in medical aid before. What shall I do? I hardly*
> *know what I write at present. He is delirious, I think, nay*
> *I almost hope, for he will hardly suffer me to approach him.*
> *For heaven's sake, throw off all other engagements and come*
> *instantly, Doctor.*
> *Yours truly,*
>
> *M.H. Wellesley*

Of course I knew this summons must be followed by prompt obedience. Without a moment's delay I ordered my carriage and departed for Wellesley House. The news was not entirely unexpected, for the last day or two paragraphs had been put forth by the public prints intimating that the Duke had returned from Adrianopolis in a very precarious state of health, and rumours had been rife in the city respecting the mysterious origin of his illness.

On my arrival I was immediately ushered into a splendid

breakfast room where I found the Duchess. All the parapher-
nalia of coffee, etc., stood before her, but it was evidently
untouched. She looked pale, faded and harassed to the last
degree. If it were not that her delicate Percyan features seem of
that perennial nature that no sickness or sorrow can take away
their loveliness, I should hardly have known her. Not the
faintest flush of carmine remained on her cheek. It was totally
colourless but at the same time exquisitely fair, and her sweet
hazel eyes were filled with a light of weary sadness that might
have drawn tears from stones. Surely, thought I, the young
Duke must be ill indeed if he cannot suffer so beautiful a
creature as this to approach him.

'Oh, Doctor,' were her first words, 'I am glad to see you! Yet
I fear even *your* skill will be in vain! It is not a common malady
by which my lord's energies have been so crushed and laid
prostrate. He himself declares that the hand that smote him
alone can cure him, and what that hand is, Heaven and the
Duke can tell but I cannot.'

'Compose yourself, my lady,' said I, for she was violently
agitated. 'You are, I fear, almost as much in want of my aid
as the Duke can be. Your affection has exaggerated his
danger. I dare swear I shall find him not near so ill as you
imagine.'

'Doctor,' she replied solemnly, 'don't say so. He is in a
strange deadly way such as I never heard of before. He
complains of burning fever in his veins, but externally he is
cold as ice. And then, what expressions, what kindling gleams
and transient ghostly clouds of feeling continually pass and
repass over his countenance! Oh, you will shudder as I do
while you watch him! And he seems, Doctor, to hate me, he
loathes me, and yet at times to struggle with his disgust. Aye,
that is what makes me so miserable as I am. But I deserve it all!

For Doctor, Doctor, if he dies I shall have been his – his murderess.'

She groaned and sank her head on her hands as she uttered this word. I knew not what to think. It seemed that *she* required my assistance whatever her royal husband might do. There was absolute insanity in the term she had made use of. I entreated her to be calm and offered her a little coffee to revive her.

She pushed the cup away and, looking at me rather wildly, said, 'Now, Dr Alford, you see what strange things come to pass. Who would have thought that Zamorna – the godlike Zamorna, our idol, the idol of me and all my sex – would have died by the hand of one of his worshippers, his chief priestess as it were. How *could* a woman do injury to him when he is so handsome, and generous, and at times so very kind. Yet it is true, I, his wife, have been his Atropos[21]. But, sir, don't think that I have literally dipped my hands in his blood, or Messalina-like[22] given him poison. No, that would be rather too bad, I should be a fiend and not a woman. By the way, sir, do you think it possible that a mere mortal woman should harden her heart by jealousy – aye, jealousy, that's the best petrifier I know of – to that extremity of stoniness that she might untrembling, unflinching, unrepenting, keeping always the image of her rival, a handsome woman perhaps, very like the beheaded Queen of Scots, full before her, that she might, thus strengthened, go to Zamorna, love on her face, and love and madness in her heart, and put into his hand a cup, drugged like the one Socrates drank,[23] and calmly see him taste it, first smiling on her, and watch that smile pass away, never to dawn more, and hear his voice as sweet as music, as sweet as that, sir' – she pulled her harp, which stood not far off, to her side and drew a single chord of the deepest and finest melody – 'and as that voice failed – but Dr Alford, I am supposing a case that never happened. You must not imagine that I did this, I only thought of it.

'One afternoon at Douro Villa, or rather one evening as I was returning from thence by moonlight, the stars in the Niger you know, sir, and all as serene as I myself might have *looked*, for I have got from my father a way of looking very quiet without, when I am furious within, at that time a dream came into my head. It haunted me all the way down the valley, that my hand might, with the thought, with proper meditation on the loveliness of Mary Stuart, and on the fidelity of her sweet miniatures, have obtained the requisite degree of steadiness to direct either a poniard to the heart of the omnipotent, or a bowl of poison to his lips. But when I got home I was told that all was done; that I had unwittingly accomplished my own intentions when I least desired it. And then, sir, I felt what I trust you may never feel, and what I think has almost turned my brain, there's a wide difference between purpose and fulfilment.'

While she talked thus I made no attempt to interrupt her. She was excited by some circumstance, apparently jealousy, to perfect frenzy. But could the subject on which her mind wandered be founded on fact – could she, in a fit of desperation – but no, impossible. Yet *she* was the daughter of Northangerland, and the Duke was known to be wild, unstable. Perhaps under all her sweet gentle semblance there might be as much passion pent as in the burning veins of her proud haughty stepmother, and if so – but I dared not pursue the supposition. With the utmost calmness of voice and manner I now proposed that she should accompany me to her lord's apartment, hoping to gain some further clue to the matter by strict observation of her deportment while in his presence.

'I'll go, Doctor,' said she, and rising quickly opened the door ere I could reach it. With a rapid unquiet step she crossed the hall before me.

We both ascended the staircase, covered with rich matting; threaded a succession of galleries, thickly carpeted; and entered a large ante-room where a dark, foreign-looking youth about fifteen years old, with coal-black eyes and hair, and very handsome though rather spare features, appeared in waiting.

'Eugene, Eugene,' said his lady, 'how is your master? Why are you not with him?'

'He ordered me out, my lady, and Finic too. Not a soul has been with him for the last half hour.'

Without reply the Duchess passed on. She softly opened the inner door, then, pausing and speaking in a scarce audible whisper, said, 'Enter first, sir, I dare not go further than the foot of the bed. He hates to see me.'

I obeyed. All was still in the wide and lofty chamber, the windows darkened with long rich drapery of crimson velvet, to which the morning sun, shining behind, gave a peculiarly vivid and brilliant appearance, the grand state bed surrounded with curtains of the same, all drooping in deeply fringed festoon folds, and sweeping the floor with their glittering gold tassels like the canopy of a royal tent. The rest of the furniture lay in dense shadow, only here and there a marble stand of silver lamps glistened as pure as snow through the gorgeous gloom by which they were encompassed. Surely, thought I, this ought to defy the darts of death if anything can. I walked to the bedside and, taking my seat in an armchair which stood near, undrew the curtain.

All the clothes, the splendid counterpane, the delicate cambric sheets, were tossed and tumbled in disorder. Lying on his back but with his face turned restlessly to the ample pillow of white velvet, appeared my noble patient. He was asleep, breathing heavily, his teeth set close, his lips a little parted, his nostrils fiercely dilating and compressing as he respired, brow darkly knit, cheek flushed with the brightest hectic, his hair coming down on his temples and curling on his forehead in rich but wild profusion. I hesitated at first whether to awake him, and the Duchess, seeing me in doubt, ventured to approach. She gazed a long time at him, and then with a moan of mingled love and agony bent down and, clasping her arms round his neck, kissed his lips and cheek with passionate tenderness. He instantly awoke. So suddenly, indeed, did his eyes flash open that I doubted whether he had been really asleep.

'White witch,' said he, earnestly regarding his lady, and gently putting her from him, 'what do you wish me to do now? Oh, to submit to a doctor! I see. Well, Alford, Death fills the room. Do you think your drugs and draughts will be noxious enough to drive him out? Open the window, sir. I am dying of suffocation and internal heat! For God's sake, remove those dark, bloody curtains! Fling the sash wide, wide up, and let me see the light! Let me feel the air!'

I did what he desired. A cool and gentle breeze immediately stole in. 'There,' said he, 'that is the kiss of the Niger. It rolls through the shrubbery without, and as it glides by my palace sends me this dewy salute in token of homage. I wish it would breathe fiercer and colder. A thundering rush of wind, roaring down the snow slopes of Elimbos, would be welcome now as glory. Henrietta Wellesley, my white witch, my seraphic hypocrite! This is better than thy embrace! By the Genii! My lady's lips burnt like fire!'

She turned on me a look of mute despair; he saw it.

'Rise up, Alford,' said he, 'and let the Queen draw near.

I have many things to say unto her and she may hear them now.'

I obeyed him; she took my seat.

'Rose of the world!' he continued. 'You have long blossomed under the palm tree's shelter, but now an axe is laid to the root thereof and the branch of protection will soon pass away. Flower, would there not be heroism in fading with thy guardian? Drink not the dew that falls at night, wave not in the breeze that blows at dawn, open not to the light that shines at noonday, then you'll soon be as withered as me. Aye, my scorching bride and her royal lover will consume to ashes in the same earth! Or what do you say to a suttee? That would be better perhaps. When I am dead, erect a pile on the shores of the Calabar; let me be carried there in state. I shall be laid on the timber. Then you, Mary, will ascend, take my head on your knee, greet my cold and bloodless lips with a few of those burning kisses – no need to apply the torches, we shall of ourselves kindle into a burst of flames so vivid that, when the inhabitants of Verdopolis look out from their casements eastward, the glow of the setting, not the rising, sun will be seen on the oriental skyline. Hah! Queen of Angria, how would you like that?'

'I would die any death with you, Adrian,' was the fond and devoted reply.

'Would you, my Percy-blossom?' said the Duke. 'No, remember, think – better to begin life on a fresh tack. The encumbrance being removed, look out for another partner. Pelham[24], you know, is still faithfully single; give your fair hand to him. It will be better worth his acceptance now that it has been joined to that of a monarch. Let him tie the second orange-flower garland on thy head that I circled with a diadem. Yield him all the rights that were mine; be gentle, obedient, dutiful to him; be keen-sighted, Mary, see that he wanders not astray. Then, doubtless, you will be happy. Happy, did I say? Hah! But there shall be a shadow in thy sunshine, Mary; a something always darkening thy sight; an eternal blot in the eye of day which no change of time, place or season can remove. I, from my grave, will haunt you by night, by morning and by noonday. I will come without sound or voice, always the same, void of variation. With no thought of burning I will stand by your side, still and motionless, with an ungrieved, unsaddened, countenance. In the hall, in the chamber, in the crowded saloon, my eye shall be ever on you. I'll follow you to your dying bed, bow above you as the wheel of existence makes its last revolution, and drink the dregs of life from lips that spoke perjury to me.'

With a look of the darkest meaning he turned on his pillow, shut his eyes, folded his arms, and was silent. The Duchess rose and left the room. I heard afterwards that she fell into a swoon on gaining her own apartment, and lay two hours without sense or motion. When she was gone I again approached him. I asked him several questions, not one of which he would answer. I attempted to feel his pulse; he pushed me from him with violence. I proposed to bleed him; but no, all was in vain. The last step, however, was absolutely necessary. His fever – or whatever it was – raged so fiercely that without some measures of mercy he would have been dead before night. Aware of his refractoriness – for this was by no means the first time I had attended him at periods of critical danger – I stepped into the antechamber and ordered Eugene Rosier to summon one or two of his master's personal attendants. Edward Laury and the dwarf, Finic, soon entered.

'Well, sir,' said the former, 'I guess the Duke is fractious?'

'Very, Ned,' returned I. 'Worse than I ever saw him before. You will have a tough job of it, but if I can once get a vein open

67

it shall soon be stopped; the loss of a few ounces of blood will soon bring him down.'

Edward nodded, and we all passed into the chamber. We had spoken low, but the ears of sick, and especially delirious, persons are often morbidly sensitive. On our entrance we found the bed and the apartment empty.

'Where is he?' said I.

'In his dressing room,' replied Rosier coolly, and, stepping to a small door covered with a curtain, he attempted to open it. It was locked. The boy uttered a low whistle and muttered with a strange kind of smile, '*Mon Dieu*, he'll surely not cut his own throat.'

I prepared to break open the door.

'Nay, Doctor,' said Laury, 'if he means to do harm to himself, we shall not mend the matter by making a din. I know the Duke, and other folk's contrariness always fixes his mind.'

This was not to be contraverted, so we stood in all the horrors of suspense about ten minutes longer. At length the door was dashed open and His Grace appeared within. He was ready dressed in his usual deep military mourning, and to a casual spectator would have appeared to be in full, vigorous health and strength. Fever, however, was burning on his cheek, and a certain dazzling and most dangerous light flickered in his eye. We all stepped back on perceiving a ready-cocked pistol grasped in either hand.

'Now, Alford,' said he, 'you will bind and bleed me now, will you? Begone, sir, instantly. My malady is nothing to you; it does not come within the limits of your confined skill. I shall no longer lie waiting the issue like a helpless child, but rise and meet Death as a man should do, face to face. The die is cast. This night the stakes will be swept away either by my hand or *his*. No inferior player shall so much as look in. So, once more,

Dr Alford, I warn you to depart quickly; the slightest attempt to oppose my will will be met by –' and he glanced at the pistols. Perceiving that coercion would only aggravate the fury of his disorder, I – for the present – thought proper to retire, first directing Edward Laury to watch his master and not on any account permit him to leave the house. I went away satisfied that *poison* had nothing to do with his illness.

2ND JULY
Read two paragraphs in the papers of today which astonished me much. The first ran thus:

> *Yesterday Mr H.M.M. Montmorency Esq. gave a splendid dinner to the heads of the Angrian Party. The Duke of Zamorna and the Earl of Northangerland were both present. His Grace appeared to be in excellent health and spirits, a circumstance which fully contradicted the reports that of late have been so industriously circulated by his enemies. We are sorry, however, to say that the Duchess is much indisposed.*

The second article was a long speech, purporting to have been delivered by the Duke on the previous night at a meeting of some scientific body, where he presided. The speech throughout was marked by his peculiar tone of eloquence. It was even more classic and elegant than usual, and had fewer of those fiery outbursts of energy (of which indeed the subject did not admit) than I ever saw in an oration of his before.

These things puzzle me. I will proceed to Wellesley House instantly and see how the case really stands.

Evening
On arriving at the young lion's magnificent den, I was shown

up first, at my own request, to the Duchess. She welcomed me eagerly.

'Ah, Doctor,' said she, 'you are come just in the right time. I was on the point of sending for you. Mr Abercrombie and Sir Astley Coleridge are both upstairs, and so are His Grace, the Duke of Wellington, and Lady Seymour. I have not been permitted to see my husband today but they say he is better. I hardly know how to believe them. Doctor, you will deal truly with me, and, if he is really convalescent, do let me have an interview with him, though it be only of ten minutes' duration.'

These words of Her Grace intimated plainly that her lord was in a dangerous, perhaps a hopeless state. They had concealed his real condition from her, perhaps in dread of its producing fatal effects. I replied evasively, but soothingly, to her request, and left the room. Edward Laury met me on the stairs.

'Did your master go out yesterday?' I immediately asked.

'Go out, sir?' was the reply. 'No, indeed. After you were gone he was worse than ever. Towards evening he grew raging mad, and, till five this morning, we had to hold him in bed by main force. Now,' continued the man calmly, but in a voice of restrained emotion, 'he may be reckoned as one that has not much more to do in this world. They are all round him waiting for the last breath as I may say.'

I passed on with an accelerated step. On pausing at the chamber door I heard a very faint sound of many whispering voices. Eugene answered to my low, scarcely audible tap. The room was darkened. A dozen persons were gathered round the bed, and two others sat at a table on which stood four lit tapers; parchment, pens and ink lay before them. I was greeted in silence. Room was directly made for me to advance, and, on taking my station with the other medical men by the pillow, I had a full view of all who were present. The Countess Seymour sat in an armchair opposite; near her stood the Duke of Wellington, the Duke of Fidena and the Earl of Northangerland. Mr Montmorency, Mr Warner, General Thornton, Viscount Castlereagh and the Earl of Arundel formed the rest of the circle. Some grave and important matter had evidently summoned them to the young monarch's dying bed. Deliberation, anxiety, earnest expectation sat on every brow, revealed dimly by the candlelight, which at this hour seemed an unnatural substitute for the broad radiance of day.

As for Zamorna, he was stretched in the midst, still and rigid as a corpse, his countenance white, his lips livid, and nothing save the motion and sparkle of his eyes indicating that he yet retained the smallest remnant of life. At my entrance, Fidena was bending over him, and the subdued sound of his voice alone broke the profound hush of the apartment.

'Zamorna,' he was saying, 'though your corporeal faculties are utterly prostrated, Heaven has, in mercy, permitted your mind to regain its balance at this last, this eleventh, hour. Once more then, I do most solemnly conjure you to settle this point while the blessing of speech remains, if you would avert the source of civil war from your kingdom. Name before all these witnesses a legal succession to the Crown you are now leaving.'

The pale lips of the royal youth trembled.

'You ask me,' he replied, in a faint but unfaltering voice, 'that which you know not. John, I am fast departing, and as soon as the shroud is round me a successor will arise without summons. Ernest follows Adrian in the number of the Kings of Angria.'

'You mean Ernest Fitz-Arthur?' abruptly interposed Northangerland, on whose countenance an ominous cloud of

71

gloom and bitterness was brooding. 'Hah! But, my lord Duke, is he your son? Is he your lawful son? Has he a legal right to the title of heir?'

A cold smile flitted across the Duke's clayey features. 'You will know in time,' he answered.

'Arthur,' pursued Fidena, 'this is a solemn hour. In the name of God, unravel this mystery! Your moments pass rapidly and none can do it save you.'

There was an interval of dead silence. Zamorna made no answer, and his face began to assume a stealing shadow.

Warner now spoke. 'I appeal to the Duke of Wellington,' he said, quickly and anxiously. 'Your Grace has yet made no attempt to extract a declaration.'

'Nor will I,' replied the Duke, determinedly. 'My son shall not have his final chance of life cut off by me.'

'Why,' began Lord Arundel, 'I think the matter is settled. Zamorna has named Fitz-Arthur and is not that enough? My heart burns to hear how you dare annoy him! By heaven, he shall die in peace if I can accomplish it! To the last drop of my blood will I defend his son's rights whether they be lawful or otherwise!'

'Silence!' said the stern Percy. 'Ernest Fitz-Arthur I say let it be, but there is a regency to appoint. Zamorna, speak once again, who shall be regent?'

'Ernest will want no regent,' answered he. 'Now I have told all, I demand rest and silence that I may gaze down on the awful gulf yawning insatiably beneath me.'

'He shall have it,' said Arundel.

'I'll stab the first man who speaks to the heart!' responded Castlereagh.

Unmoved, Northangerland went on. 'Who shall be regent?' he repeated. 'Pronounce quickly, Monarch. If you die and make no sign on the subject, woe to Angria. Let a voice of lamentation be heard on every hearth, in every household. The sword of war is unsheathed and the blade will rankle in many a bosom ere Adrian be cold in his grave.'

'Bad and remorseless man!' said the Duke of Fidena, in a tone of roused indignation. 'Is this language for a deathbed, for your son-in-law's, for a monarch's, for Zamorna's deathbed? I will hear no more of it, my lord! He *shall* breathe his last calmly! Arthur, my dear Arthur, turn from this world to a better. Great God! I trust a happy light shines above your path onward.'

'John,' said the Prince, 'there is no light. The river of death alone rolls before me and its waters are pitchy dark, but I can cross them without dread, without a shudder. Is it noon?'

'Five minutes are yet to elapse,' replied the peculiarly harsh and grating voice of one of the notaries at the table.

Suddenly the Duke started up in his bed. The effect of this action was like the spring of a galvanised corpse.

'Wretch!' he exclaimed, with frightful energy of voice and manner. 'Art thou there? Then I feel as if I could live still! I will defy, I will vanquish thee at last! Grapple with me, now, hand to hand, and see who shall be conqueror! Five minutes yet to elapse. I thought the hour was long gone by. Courage! Hope, Zamorna! A star yet glimmers. She will not, dare not, be faithless.' The notary answered by a hollow laugh.

'I hear a sound,' continued the Duke, bending his head. 'Far off, light, rapid; no other ear can take it in. It is her tread, her own sweet fairy tread. Villain, tremble! My champion comes at last.'

'The wheels of her chariot tarry,' said the notary, rising and approaching the window. 'I look through the lattice, and no woman's robe flutters in the wind. But St Augustine's clock shows its hand on the doomed hour. A warning of her hero's departure has, by this time, rung through all Verdopolis.'

He was silent. Every quickened ear at that moment heard a footstep. The chamber door trembled; it seemed to split asunder, so impetuously was it burst open. A lady swept in. Her motion was as swift, almost as noiseless, as lightning. Instinctively we all fell back. She sank on her knees by the bedside and hid her face in the hand which Zamorna stretched towards her.

'Ransomed,' was the only word whispered by her parting lips. The mingling bells of the city just then struck the first toll of twelve. She rose as they concluded, turned round, regarded us all with a keen, penetrating glance of her fine black eyes.

'Gentlemen,' she said, with a blush partly of excitement, and partly, as it appeared, of anger, 'I hope you will not think of remaining here. There is no need of successions being settled now. Zamorna will not die and this gloomy chamber is darkened for nothing.'

She stepped to each window in turn, hastily removed all the blinds and curtains with which they were shrouded, flung up the lattices, extinguished the candles, ordered the remaining notary to depart – one of them was already gone we know not how – in a quick passionate voice, which he was not slow in obeying, and then again glanced impatiently at us.

'All this requires an explanation, young woman,' said the Earl of Northangerland.

'It does, my lord,' she replied, curtsying very deferentially, 'but perhaps you will allow the explanation to be postponed till my master can himself decide whether he chooses it to be given or not.'

'Mina,' said the Duke of Wellington. She started when

he spoke, and the colour mounted brightly to her cheeks; immediately she was at his feet, kneeling on one knee with her head bowed on the other.

'What brought you here, my little girl?' asked the Duke, in his kindliest tone.

'My lord,' she answered, 'if I am an intruder, I will return, but this morning Finic informed me that my presence might be useful to, to, to my late lady's son. And dared I sit still when *he* required that I should be active?'

'I fear you would not,' said His Grace. 'However, you are a good child, and this morning's work adds another debt to those he already owes you. He'll pay it as he did the former.'

Miss Laury shrunk as if she had been crushed to the earth. Her head dropped so low that the jetty curls rested in clusters on the carpet.

'Go and serve him, Mina,' continued the Duke, 'spend your life in his Egyptian bondage.[25] His chains, I see, are locked on every limb.'

'They are,' she said, rising proudly, 'and no hand but that of Death shall rend them off. His born thrall I am and will be.'

The medical gentlemen, who meantime had been examining Zamorna, now pronounced that an astonishing and most miraculous change had taken place for the better. Something like warmth had been communicated to the blood which was again circulating freely. The pulse could now be felt; the heart had resumed its action; and the livid shadow had vanished from his face.

The deep suppressed joy of Miss Laury at this intelligence was such as I have seldom seen. She came and hung over him, and gazed into his eyes as if all of the universe she cared for was contained in their dark shining spheres. It seemed as if she thought she had acquired a right to look at him undaunted, as if, for the moment, she felt he was hers by redemption. The feeling, however, scarcely appeared in her countenance before it vanished, and then again she was the doomed slave of infatuation, devoted, stricken, absorbed in one idea, finding a kind of strange pleasure in bearing the burden and carrying the yoke of him whose fascinations fettered her so strongly. The end of her being, the pride of her life seemed to consist in labouring, drudging for Zamorna. He grasped her hand and smiled upon her most sweetly, and said something in a tone of the gentlest condescension. *That*, I dare say, repaid the silly girl a hundredfold.

All now except the Duke of Wellington, the Countess Seymour, Mina, Rosier and Finic left the room. As we were descending the staircase I happened to linger a little behind on one of the landing places. Someone called me by name; it was Edward Laury. He stood leaning against the wall, his arms folded, his handsome face flushed, his dark eyes glancing from under his knit brows. The resemblance between daughter and father struck me forcefully.

'Doctor,' he asked, 'is not Mina Laury come?'

I answered affirmatively.

'Curse it!' said he. 'I wish the girl had half wit, and I wish too that Duke of Zamorna had half honesty. I would hate him if I could, but then he's my king, and besides I taught him to shoot and to hunt. He was a brave, a bonnie lad, and a finer finger never touched trigger. If it hadn't been for that, if he hadn't walked by my side many a long day, many a moonlit night, over moors and along deer tracks and wood walks, I'd long since have riddled his bones with either cold steel or hot lead. I was a fool and waur[26] than a fool ever to harbour him in my bit of a hut. I knew he was wild and heartless – heartless, that is, in some things – and yet I must needs take the viper

76

into my very home-close[27] and warm it on my hearth. I've drank his venom since for my pains and yet I still stick to him, and like him, and would e'en most die for him. Idiot that I am! *I'm* not a woman! What for, then, can't I get his blood and run for it?'

'I have no doubt you have your reasons for acting in a better and wiser manner,' replied I, wishing to soothe him.

'Reasons! I've no reasons but his own witchery. You know, Doctor, how he behaved when I was wounded at the Battle of Velino. He made me lie in his own quarters, on his own campbed. He examined my wound every day himself, and often when the surgeons were busy, dressed it. At night he used to wrap his cloak round him and lie down on the floor and, whatever I said, would continue to do so till I was quite well. Then he forced me to drink wine from his mess table; I had my rations from my general's canteens. He screened me in that tough matter about Sir John Flower, now Lord Richton, and once in a hard tussle of three to one he saved my life at the hazard of his own. With all this it's impossible for me to detest him – at least not long together. Besides we are both Irishers in a way, and they never bear malice. Yet, spite of all, I can't abide him at this moment, so I'll off to the west till my blood cools.' He struck the butt-end of a long fowling piece, which he held in his hand, violently against the ground, dashed downstairs, and disappeared in the hall below.

On entering the saloon, to which the other gentlemen had withdrawn, I found them all departed except Northangerland. He was sitting on a sofa near his daughter and conversing with her earnestly. Supposing myself an intruder I was about to retire; the Earl called me back.

'Doctor,' said he, 'the Duchess is anxious to see her kind, considerate husband; what do you say to the matter? The rest of the medical people have put their wise veto upon it.'

'I fear,' replied I, 'I shall be compelled to agree with them. Her Grace suffered too much in the last interview to hazard another so quickly.'

'Well,' said she with a sigh, 'I must submit then, I suppose, but after this day no earthly command except his own shall keep me from him.'

The Earl rose and beckoned me to a recess.

'Alford,' he commenced abruptly, 'I wish to know how long Zamorna has been ill.'

'For the four last days he has never quitted the house,' said I.

'A downright falsehood, sir!' returned Northangerland. 'How dare you say so, when yesterday I saw him at Montmorency Hotel in much better health than you ever restored a patient to in your life. He accompanied me after dinner to Ellrington House, and afterwards, like a fool, escorted the Countess to some absurd assembly of scientific idiots, where, according to her account, he was particularly brilliant.'

'So I read, my lord, in the papers, and I assure you the intelligence staggered me. For proof of my assertion I refer Your Lordship to the Duchess.'

'I need no reference,' said he, 'for she told me the same tale before your entrance and I thought grief had somewhat affected her brain. That opinion is now transferred to you. Don't think to persuade me out of my senses, sir. I tell you, the Duke of Zamorna was in my company all yesterday afternoon and part of the evening. He looked, talked, laughed and swaggered as usual, and I was never more surprised in my life than when this morning a note from Mr Maxwell summoned me to attend his dying bed. Then the sudden turn in his health, the behaviour of the notary, the arrival of that girl – By the bones of Scylla[28], it's an infernal affair altogether.' So saying, His Lordship left the room. The Duchess had already quitted it, so I summoned my carriage and returned home.

CHAPTER SIX

Five days elapsed. During that time Zamorna, under the tender care of Mina Laury and the skilful superintendence of Dr Alford, rapidly recovered his almost annihilated health. The Duchess, at his own request, at length received permission to see him. She was sitting at breakfast when Eugene entered and put into her hands a small twisted billet written in pencil. The hand was her husband's and the welcome words as follows:

Come to me, Mary, as soon as you will. Alford thinks an interview now not only allowable but advisable. He says you are pining to a shadow. I fear much, my sweetest, that your love has been ill-requited by me during my moments of delirium. What I said I neither know nor wish to know. Only a confused and frightful dream remains in my mind, whose details I should abhor fully to recall. I'll make up for it hereafter, so come quickly. You will find me alone in my dressing room. I am just apparelled and have dismissed Finic.

Yours tenderly and truly,

Adrian

Up started the Duchess, nearly upsetting the rosewood stand with its burden of priceless porcelain. She flew to the door and through the hall and was just placing her foot on the stairs when a note or two of music arrested her attention. It was the tremulous vibration of a guitar, lightly and carelessly yet skilfully touched. The sounds proceeded from one of the numerous saloons whose groined portals arched the walls around her. Who could it be? She knew the style, it was familiar to her. Could the Duke – but no, impossible. Again she listened, the tune rose: a wild, soft, melancholy air, monotonous, but exquisitely plaintive. It trembled, swelled, died away, breathed into life again, uttered its low lingering close, and gave place to silence.

'As I live,' said Mary, 'that is his hand! My ear is practised and cannot mistake what it has so often drunk in with delight.' She stood irresolute. There was a slight shock in the circumstance of hearing sounds so unexpected echoing from a part of the house just opposite to where she imagined her lord to be – something that ruffled her nerves, more so indeed than such a trivial thing would seem to warrant. Again the strings were swept and the notes of an extravaganza – just such as the Duke is accustomed to run extempore when he happens by chance to take up his instrument – stole in quivering and liquid melody through the hall. Still the Duchess hesitated. She felt in a manner chained to the spot, but a sudden cessation of sound loosed the spell. She started, hastened to the saloon, whose partially unclosed folding door had permitted egress to the music, slid it further back and entered. Zamorna was there sure enough. He stood at a table near the upper end of the room; his guitar lay beside him, and while he turned over the leaves of a large and splendidly bound volume, he carelessly hummed the words of the tune he had just played.

Mary paused to contemplate him. No appearance of ill-health, no trace of recent indisposition lingered on his kingly countenance. There was none of that languor and feebleness in his attitude or aspect which usually marks the upriser from a sickbed. His complexion had all the fine glowing clearness which it ever wears in perfect health, and his eyes were full and bright and hawk-like, as if the quenching power of fever had never touched them.

'Death has for me been merciful,' said Henrietta, as she came forward. 'His shadow has passed away and left my noble and beautiful idol as glorious as it found him.'

The Duke, of course, looked up. It was a curious glance he gave his lady. The vermilion lip was bit as if to suppress the half-comic smile that mantled round it; the eyebrow was raised. The light of the eye was arch, scrutinising, rather satirical yet kind enough; it forbad fear, yet did not invite any of that overflowing tenderness with which Mary was inclined to greet him. She stood silent, blushing and embarrassed.

'My dear Arthur,' at last she faltered out, 'why do you keep me at such a distance? Why are you so cool and strange? I *wish* I knew the reason! It should be the business of my life to labour night and day until I earned some portion of a warmer affection.'

'I am not angry with you, Mary,' replied Zamorna, 'not I. Indeed, quite the contrary. I love you well enough, but, you little witch, what brought you to Douro Villa that evening?'

'To speak the truth, Adrian, it was curiosity. I wanted to see whether Miss Laury was so handsome, and Fitz-Arthur so like you, as people said.'

'Well, Mary,' taking her hand, 'and what do you think? Is the girl a pretty one? Don't be jealous now. I solemnly swear to you that I never spoke more than three words at a time, and those of the most commonplace kind, to her in my life. She's in other hands than mine, I assure you, and if I were to come so near to her as I do now to you, such a hubbub would be raised that the Tower of All Nations there would rock to its foundations. So speak freely, do you think her pretty?'

'Very pretty,' sighed poor Mary. 'And Ernest and little Emily, very, very like.'

The Duke laughed. 'Aye, so they are,' said he. 'It can't be denied. But cheer up, Mary, cheer up, the time may come when you'll not sorrow for that likeness.'

The Duchess shook her head. Tears began to steal down her fair pale cheeks. Encouraged, however, by his manner, which was gentle and friendly, though perhaps not loving, she ventured to insinuate her hand, which he held only by the tips of the fingers, further into his. An expression, at that moment, crossed his countenance such as she had never seen on her lord's face before. An odd, indescribable, mischievous mixture of feelings which, while it lasted, seemed almost to change the features. At the same time he pinched her hand very hard, rather unkindly, so that the rings on her finger pressed against the bone and she uttered a faint exclamation of pain. Instantly the door was flung open; in bounced the ungainly figure of Finic. His small and beast-like optics glared in his head like Roman candles; he mouthed, gesticulated and capered furiously. The Duke first laughed, then hit him a sound stunning blow; he walked to the window, threw it up, sprang through the aperture and vanished among the trees of the shrubbery without.

'What brought you here, Finic?' said Mary, turning angrily to the dwarf.

He fell down before her, his hands crossed on his bosom, and his forehead touching the carpet at her feet.

'I will have no mummery!' she continued, forgetting in her displeasure that he could not understand her. 'Your conduct is very insolent, very unaccountable! No sooner have I spoken three words with my lord alone than you must enter and disturb our conversation! What do you mean? I can endure it no longer! But poor miserable wretch, I might as well talk to a statue. Let go my dress, sir!' She snatched it from him, as his long thin fingers closed slowly on the folds, and, heedless of the low wail of entreaty which he sent after her, quitted the saloon.

Eugene Rosier met her at the door. This encounter did not greatly soothe her ruffled feelings. She was in that mood (a very unusual one with her) which finds cause of irritation in every occurrence.

'What!' said she. 'Listening, I suppose, to see that I don't overstep the bounds of decorum! This is a strange state of things! I do not comprehend it and I will not bear it! Pray, sir, is it by your master's orders that I am watched so by yourself and that abortive wretch?'

'My master, madam,' replied Eugene, with a look of surprise, 'he has given me no orders, except that he wishes to know whether you could read his billet.'

'Read his billet? Yes, sir, and I have obeyed the intimation which it contained. But I might as well have remained in my own apartment, he will scarcely speak to me.'

Eugene drew up his mouth as if for a whistle. Respect for his lady, however, appeared to restrain him.

'Madam,' said he, 'the Duke desires to learn the reason of your not having visited him in his dressing room, that's the short and long of the matter.'

'You will drive me past my patience!' returned the Duchess. 'I have visited him; he was in that saloon a minute ago and by his manner did not seem to want, or even to expect me much.'

The page stood silent an instant. He seemed confounded, but presently a wink of the eye and a roguishly significant smile told that he had solved the riddle to his satisfaction.

'Hah, my lady,' he went on. 'His Grace, if I might venture to say so, has queer moods sometimes, but if you'll just step upstairs now, I'll wager my royal livery to a dustman's jacket, he'll meet you in a different temper.'

As Rosier spoke, a cough was heard within the saloon just like the Duke's.

'He is come back,' said Mary, 'I'll venture to try him again.'

She was about to open the door, when Eugene, with a temerity which he had never before ventured to display, coolly removed her hand from the lock, placed himself between her and the closed portal, and stood confronting her with a face whose boldness said plainly enough, 'You shall not re-enter this room if I can help it.'

She stepped back, perfectly astounded at his impudence. Before she could speak a yell of Finic's arose, then a laugh, the well-known 'Ha! Ha!' of Zamorna, and then an equally well-known voice exclaimed: 'Mary, fight your way through all obstacles. I am here, and I command you to come unto me.'

She sprang again to the door, again she grasped the handle.

'Madam,' said Rosier, 'I beg, I entreat, I implore, my lady, I supplicate that you will hear me one instant,' but no, she was deaf to his remonstrances. He then dismissed his face of prayer and humility, assumed a natural aspect of unblushing hardihood, drew up his slight but sinewy frame to its full height and, seizing both her hands, said, 'Now, my lady, will you go upstairs? If you say, yes, I'll fall on my knees and beg pardon for what I've already done. If you say, no, I must, I really must try my strength further. It's as much as my life is worth to lay a finger on you, but it's more than my life is worth to permit a second interview today. The Duke may stab me for hindering you, but he'll certainly blow my brains out if I don't hinder you.'

With quivering lips, death-white cheeks, and a blighting glance of passion the Duchess broke from him and moved away. She was now the true image of her father. There was absolute malignity in the bitterness and scorn of the look she flung on her presumptuous page.

'*Mon Dieu!*' said he, as the haughty sweep of her robes passed by him. '*C'est fait de moi*;[29] she'll never forgive me, this comes of being over-zealous. I wish I'd let the Duke and her meet and manage it together. But then, the after-reckoning – and he's so mischievous. Why did he call out? *Parbleu*, that made her quite unmanageable! But she's off now, so I must try and be beforehand with explaining.' So saying, he skipped across the hall and up the staircase with his customary agility.

Mary retired to her chamber. She sat down, leant her white face on her whiter hands, and for half an hour continued utterly motionless. At length a low tap came to the door. She made no answer but it opened and in sailed the figure of a tall gentlewoman clothed in rustling black silk. She raised her head. 'Temple, why am I disturbed in this manner? Am I not to be safe from intrusion even in my own chamber?'

'My dear lady,' said the matron, 'you have been vexed, I see, or you would not be angry with me for coming at the Duke's command to tell you he desires your company in his dressing room.'

'Dressing room again!' replied the Duchess. 'How often is that word to be sounded in my ears? I say he is not in his dressing room, and, Temple, I wonder you should bring me messages with which you were never charged. He does not wish to see me!' and now the spoilt child broke out. The young Duchess burst into tears. She sobbed and wept, and reiterated two or three times, 'I won't go! He never sent for me! He hates me.'

'My lady, my lady,' continued Mrs Temple, in a tone of alarm, 'for heaven's sake don't try him any more. He is not angry yet, but I dread to see that look of placidity begin to settle about his lips. Do take my arm, madam, for you are very much agitated, and let us go before the cloud gathers.'

'Well, well, Temple,' said Mary, for she could not long keep up that angry mood towards her servants which was so unnatural to her cheerful, indulgent temper. 'I may perhaps go soon if you'll let me alone. But then he does not want me, and that hideous dwarf Finic, and that insolent boy Eugene will break in upon us, and he will let them insult me as they like. No, Temple, I won't go! I won't go!'

'Nay, my dearest lady, think it over again. If I return with that message he'll just say, "Very well, Temple, my respects to your lady, and say I am sorry I troubled her," and then he'll sit down and look like his bust in your cabinet there, and it will be many a long day before he asks to see you again.'

The Duchess returned no answer to this reasoning, but at last she rose slowly and, still weeping and with evident reluctance, resigned herself to the conduct of the worthy housekeeper, who, respectfully yet affectionately soothing and supporting her gentle mistress, led her from the room and on towards the Duke's apartments. They entered the hated dressing room. The omnipresent Zamorna was as certainly there as he had been in the saloon, but he wore a different mood, a different aspect. Wan and wasted was the tall thin form, seated by the hearth at a table covered with books. His head with all its curls rested on a woefully attenuated hand; his brow was blanched, whitened with sickness, his cheek worn and hollow and his full, floating eyes lit with languid light the learned page on which they rested. A portrait of the Duchess of Wellington hung over the mantelpiece – how like his mother looked her glorious son!

'Well, Temple,' said he, roused by their approaching footsteps, 'you have been most successful after all, I see.

Woman to woman, they know how to manage each other best! But, bless me, what is the matter? Tears, sobs, Mary? Look up, love.'

But Mary would not look up. She shrunk from him as he advanced and was going to take her from the care of Mrs Temple, turned away her face, and actually gave him a slight repulse with her hand. He was silent a minute. The awful calmness came over his before gentle countenance.

'Annabel,' said he to the housekeeper, 'explain! Your mistress seems capricious.'

'Oh, she will be better directly, my lord,' replied Mrs Temple. 'My lady,' in an undertone, 'pray think what you are about. I do implore you not to trifle with your own happiness.'

'I am not trifling with my own happiness,' sobbed the Duchess. 'If he touches me, those hateful satellites of his will be on us directly, and he will leave the room, and I must remain to hear and endure what insolence they choose to favour me with.'

'Madness,' muttered Mrs Temple. 'I never saw you in such a way before, my lady.'

'Annabel, trouble yourself no further with remonstrances,' said the Duke. 'Assist your lady back to her own room.'

He resumed his seat, again leant his head on his hand, and in a moment appeared to be thoroughly absorbed in the study which had before occupied his attention. A sense of remorse seemed now to touch the Duchess. She looked at him and for the first time perceived how pale and thin and languid sickness had left him. Immediately there was a strong revulsion of feeling; tears flowed more rapidly than ever; her neck and bosom swelled with the choking sobs that forced their way one after the other. The waywardness of the indulged child of aristocracy took a different turn. She pushed

Mrs Temple off when she offered to lead her from the chamber, went to her husband and stood beside him, trembling and weeping violently. He did not long remain unmoved by her anguish, but, soon rising, led her to a sofa, and, sitting down by her, wiped her tears with his own handkerchief.

'Annabel,' said he, 'you may go. I think we shall be right in time.'

The excellent gentlewoman smiled, but as old Bunyan says, 'the water stood in her eyes'[30]; as she went out she remarked with the freedom of a favourite retainer, 'Now, my lord, don't be placid. Don't be like your bust.'

'I won't, Annabel,' said he, then, with the softest smile and sweetest tone, he turned to his lady and continued, 'Well, Maria *piangendo*[31], when is this shower to be succeeded by sunshine?'

She made no answer, but the radiant spheres under her arched brows were already flashing more cheerfully through their diamond rain.

'Ah,' said he, 'I see it will clear up, there is a light already on the horizon. Now, my love, why have you delayed so long complying with the request contained in my billet?'

'*Dear, dear* Arthur, have you forgot that I met you in the crimson saloon scarcely half an hour since? And you would hardly touch me, and spoke and looked so strangely, quite different to what you do now – you seemed not so pale, not so wasted.'

'Handsomer, I dare say,' interrupted he with something of a sneer.

'No, Arthur, I love you far better now. But I cannot tell how the difference is: my eyes must have been unaccountably bewildered; you appeared healthy and fresh and vigorous.

I never saw you more so in my life, and these hands, Oh my lord, the flesh has fallen strangely from your fingers. They could not retain your rings, and yet I perfectly recollect that as you once or twice passed them across your forehead, the sunshine fell on them and they sparkled most brilliantly with jewels.'

The Duke looked disturbed. 'Stuff, child,' said he, 'you are dreaming.'

'Impossible, Arthur, here is ocular demonstration. Do you remember pressing my hand very hard?'

'Pressing your hand very hard!' said he, starting up. 'What business had you to come so near me? Pray, madam, was I very kind? Very cordial? Very loving? By heaven, if you say yes –' He paused; something seemed to agitate him greatly.

'No, my lord, you were not indeed. Your coldness made me very unhappy, and when you squeezed my hand, it seemed rather in anger than kindness, for those marks remained as a token.' She showed him the fingers a little bruised where the rings had rubbed against them.

'Right,' said he, 'that gives me pleasure, and yet it was most rudely and roughly done. How could I hurt such a fair and delicate hand?' and snatching it he pressed it warmly to his lips. Mary smiled through her tears.

'You do not utterly hate me then, my noble Adrian?' said she, but with a look of alarm. 'Where is Finic? Will he not be interfering presently?'

'Not now, not now, Mary. But I wish to know, love, what words I made use of during that mysterious interview in the crimson saloon? Don't be surprised at my question. This whole affair must now to you appear thoroughly incomprehensible, but some time the mist may clear up. How in the first place did I receive you?'

'Very coldly, Arthur. I was prepared to throw my arms round you, but it would not do. The first look dashed and miserably confounded me. It was like cold water flung on boiling oil.'

'Right,' said the Duke. 'But go on. On what subjects did I converse?'

'You asked me among other things whether I thought Mina Laury pretty, and you told me not to be jealous, for that you had never spoken above three words at a time to her in your life.'

The Duke coughed significantly and turned away his face. It was covered with as deep a glow as the blood could now communicate to his blanched complexion.

'Did you believe me, Mary?' he asked in a low tone. She sighed and shook her head. 'Well, proceed.'

'The next thing you enquired whether I thought Fitz-Arthur like you. I said yes, and little Emily too, for indeed, my lord, they are your very miniatures.'

'Curse it!' said he, speaking between his teeth. 'I'll hear no more. Why did he, *I* – I mean – talk such infernal nonsense? Wrong-headed scapegrace! But I'll be even with him! Time for Finic to interfere and Eugene too. I say, Mary, whenever you find me in that absurd mood, revenge yourself by giving me a smart box on the ear. Do not fear either retaliation or any very lasting anger. Do it, love, I command you, and a kiss, a hundred kisses shall be your reward when I come to my right senses.'

Mary smiled at him and leant her head on his shoulder. 'Arthur,' said she, 'I begin to think that you have a double existence. I am sure the Zamorna I saw in the saloon is not the Zamorna who now sits by me. That cared little for me; this, I will believe – nay, I am sure – loves me; that was strong and in full flourish; this droops at present. But to my eyes, the pale lips that now smile on me are dearer a thousand, a million, times than those ruby ones that sneered at me an hour ago. These fingers feel and look very thin, but I love them far better than the white and rounded hand that lately crushed mine in its scornful clasp. Yet what am I talking about? There cannot be two Zamornas on this earth; it would not hold them! My brain is surely turned to entertain the idea for an instant! Ridiculous, impossible, chimerical! You will think me mad, Adrian!'

He laughed wildly, sweetly, but not heartily. 'Bless thee,' said he, 'I am madder myself, I think. However, no more of this just now, it is a dangerous subject. Yet the spell must be dissolving. A week ago a third part of what I have listened to patiently today would have killed me, either with passion or horror. Leave me for the present, love, I must reconsider the events of the morning.'

He clasped her to him, kissed her tenderly, and then rose and led her to the door. She slowly, reluctantly left him. Never before had he been so deeply dear to her as now. There was something inexpressibly touching in the aspect of his stately form and noble countenance deprived of their customary brightness, but invested with a mild, wan, melancholy fascination that heretofore had been wholly foreign to him. At least of late years, for at the ages of sixteen, seventeen, eighteen and nineteen, when he was a slender, delicate-complexioned boy, thin as a lath from his rapid growth, his manners were much gentler than they are now. How has he altered since twenty! There was no grandeur in his form till that time, no martial majesty in his features. He looked elegant and effeminate and contemplative, and more like an extremely tall and beautiful girl than a bold, blustering man. Yes, hear it, ye ladies of Africa, the Duke of Zamorna was once like a girl! That assertion seems incredible now when we look at the fiery, haughty, imperious face of the young satrap of Angria with its quenchless, transfixing glances and rapid changes of expression in which every turn only displays pride, effrontery, and impetuosity in new and continually varied lights. He once never showed those vices except when he was angered. And truly, Lord Douro, at the age of twelve, caught up in a whirlwind of passion, bore an appalling resemblance to the Duke of Zamorna at the age of twenty-two. In the same tantrums, how the violet veins on his white brow and whiter neck swelled and throbbed; how the clustering brown curls were tossed from their resting places on forehead and temple, like the forelock of a prancing stallion; his slight pliant form would strain and writhe while he struggled with his opponent (commonly Quashia) as though the spirit strove in mortal agony to accomplish that by force of desire which its clay casket was unequal to from fragility.

I could talk much of those times, but at present I must continue what I have now in hand. Reader, pass to the next chapter, if you are not asleep.

CHAPTER SEVEN

The Vale of Verdopolis! That has a sweet yet kindling sound. The Nile-swept Vale of Egypt, the rose-strewn Vale of Persia, both hold grand and gorgeous and delicate scenes in the hollows of their mighty bosoms, but is Cairo like the Queen of Nations? Are Candahar and Ispahan[32] like the emporium of the world? No, dear Reader. You will think from this preamble that I am going to give a panorama description of our valley in all its glory, all its amplitude; to tell how the wide, bright billows of the Niger roll through banks that look down in magnificent serenity on their own tree-dropped verdure, sloping into the illimitable depths of skies like oceans, skirted with fertile shores, crossed with the rippling river waves, clouded with vanishing foam as pure and transient as snow wreaths. If this is your fear, dismiss it. I merely ask you to alight with me from the six o'clock morning coach, rattling northward over a road like a sea beach, equally broad, equally even. Cry on the jarvey[33] to draw in just where that pleasant shady branch road makes itself independent of the main one. I am going to breakfast at Douro Villa and choose, instead of entering at that vast, granite gateway, which proudly opens a passage through the huge and impregnable park wall, and so going straight along the carriage road, winding amid grove, and lawn, and avenue, and open park, even to the villa two miles up the country – I choose, I say, instead of following this track, to take a cut across some pleasant fields I know of, to which this tree-girdled bypath will conduct me.

Having reached the second field, I sat down at a stile over which two lofty beeches hung their embowering branches. It was very delightful, being early morning, the air cool and fresh, the grass green and dewy, the flowers in the hedgerows exhaling their sweetest perfumes. A little rill wandered along down the sides of the pasture fields, and plenty of primroses, of wood sorrel with their clustering leaves and faintly tinted blossoms, of vetches, wild hyacinths and geraniums budded in blushing beauty on the borders. All was breathlessly still, that is, so far as regards the tumultuous voice of humanity, for there were thrushes singing on the treetops, skylarks warbling in the air, and rooks cawing from the rookery of Girnington Hall, which was seen at a distance. The last sound was not the least musical to my ears: it gave a sequestered country effect to the whole landscape which I could feel and enjoy but not express. I chose this situation to rest at because it afforded a most lovely prospect of Douro Villa. The hedge under which I sat was quickset and formed the boundary to the park on this side. The deer could not overleap it because it was planted much higher than their pastures and formed the summit of a natural wall eight feet high. Leaning against a leafy bough of the beech trees, as I sat on the stile which they canopied, I could in luxurious ease contemplate all the beauty spread beneath me. Far, far down the grounds declined in vast slopes of verdure, varied by large stately trees, brushed by the light feet of gambolling stags, who, wild with the delicious freshness and fragrance of the morning, were bounding in all directions. As the huge dell descended, the foliage thickened till it became a wood in the centre, and up from its Eden bowers started the columns, the portico, and the classic casements of the fair Grecian villa, all lifted to the early sunshine by a low knoll of shaven lawn and pleasure ground, whose light, delicate green contrasted beautifully with the darker verdure of the park and woods. Nothing could be sweeter, more elegant, more Elysian. It had not the aspect of a fine old family seat, but it seemed like the abode of taste and refinement and princely pride.

No landscape is complete without figures, and my pencil, or rather pen, shall now depict one or two of these animating adjuncts on the canvas. Slowly mounting the flowery hill on whose summit I was posted, I saw a fair and youthful lady. She was without bonnet. Her glowing cheek and raven curls announced Mina Laury. A little child lay in her arms, and another, Ernest Fitz-Arthur, ran on before her. Both of these were likewise uncovered; their ringlets danced in the morning wind, and their lovely cherub faces glowed with pleasure and exercise. Ernest was on the brow presently. He flung himself down immediately under the wall of turf when he reached it.

'Come, Mina,' he exclaimed, 'make haste, make haste! I can see all the road through the valley from here, but Papa is not coming yet. There are plenty of people and plenty of horses and some carriages covering it like little specks, but I shall know Papa by his plume when he comes, and that is not to be seen at present.'

Mina soon arrived at his post of observation. She likewise sat down and placed the little gazelle-eyed creature she carried on the grass beside her. It leant its cheek against her smooth satin dress and looked up at her so eagerly and animatedly as if it would have spoken.

'Emily wants Mama,' said Fitz-Arthur. 'And, Mina, why doesn't she come out this beautiful morning? She might, you know, with Blanche and Harriet and have a long walk in the park before Papa comes.'

'She is in her oratory, my lord,' replied Miss Laury, 'and so are her gentlewomen. But we shall see her walking on the lawn after prayers are over, I dare say.'

'Father Gonsalvi makes her pray a long while, I think,'

continued Ernest. 'I should not like to be a Roman Catholic, and Papa says I am not to be. But Emily will, and then she'll have to tell her beads every night and confess each week. I hate that confession worst of all. If Father Gonsalvi were to ask me what sins I'd committed I would rather bite out my tongue than tell him, wouldn't you, Mina?'

She smiled. 'Father Gonsalvi is a good man, my lord,' replied she, 'but I am not of his faith, and so it would be a hard thing to make me kneel before him in the confessional.'

'That's right, Mina. Do you know Zamorna has ordered him never to trouble you with trying to make you believe in saints and holy water?'

'What?' said Mina blushing. 'Did the Duke speak about me, did he think it worth his while –' She stopped.

'Yes, yes,' replied Ernest very simply. 'Zamorna loves you dearly. I don't believe you think so, Mina, by your sorrowfulness, but I am sure he does. You had just been in the room for something and had gone out, and he looked at Gonsalvi very sternly and said, "Holy Father, that is a lamb that can never be gathered to the one true fold. Sir, Miss Laury is mine. Therefore, take notice, she cannot be a disciple of our blessed Mother Church. You understand me?" and Mama's priest smiled in his quiet way and bowed low, but afterwards I saw him biting his lip, and that is a sure sign of anger with him.'

Mina answered not. Her thoughts, indeed, seemed to have wandered from the prattle of her little comforter to other and distant reminiscences, and for the moment the happy light on her countenance told that they had found rest. How touching was that interval of silence. All calm sunshine around, nothing heard but the tinkle of the hidden rivulet, the warbling of a lark unseen in ether, and the rustle of foliage wind-borne from the bottom of the dell where a belt of forest trees waved round the Palladian villa.

Ernest spoke again. 'Mina,' said he, 'people say Zamorna, when he was as old as me, was just like what I am now. And don't you think when I am as old as him I shall be like what he is?'

'I believe you will, my lord, in mind as well as in person.'

'Well then, Mina, never look sad any more, for I promise solemnly I'll marry you.'

Miss Laury started. 'What do you mean, child?' said she, with a look of surprise and a somewhat forced laugh.

'I mean,' he returned quite seriously, 'that you would like to marry Zamorna, and so, as I shall be just like Zamorna, I shall do as well, and as he won't marry you, I will.'

'Nonsense, child, you know not what you are talking about. Pray, my Lord Ravenswood, say no more on the subject. You will make me sadder than ever if you do.'

'Not I,' was the answer. 'You *shall*, I am determined, you *shall* be Countess of Ravenswood, and we will live together at Castle Oronsay, for twenty years hence that will be mine, you know, and I am sure, Mina, you would like that castle. It has a loch all round it and great hills, far higher than any we see here, some of them black in winter and purple in summer, and some of them covered with woods filled with dark close-set trees called pines. The rooms at Oronsay are not like these at Douro Villa. They have no marble on the walls or floor, and not such light open windows. They will seem to frown at you when you first enter them, and the hall is hung with pictures of men in armour and women in whalebone that in dark days and towards twilight look terribly grim, but you must not be afraid. They can do no harm. They are only painted. And then there are chambers in the west wing with handsomer and younger faces set in gold frames, and these are all hung with velvet, and they look out onto the castle esplanade. And, Mina, you shall sit with me by the lattices cut deep into walls as thick and solid as rocks, and in stormy days we'll watch how the clouds curl round Ben Carnach, and how the mist and rain settles on his head, and listen to the distant muttering far off among the cliffs of Arderinis. When that is heard it's a sign that there's a strong blast coming, and soon you see it bending all the trees as it roars down Glen Avon; foam bursts in the water under us, and all the waves of Loch Sunart seem to break in one rush at the foot of the castle walls. Oh, I delight in such times as those, and so you will, I am sure! Now be Lady Ravenswood! Do, Mina, and you don't know how much I'll love you.'

'Beginning in good time, my boy,' said a voice close beside me, and at the same instant someone laid his hand on my shoulder, bounded over the hedge and the eight feet of turf wall, and alighted just before Mina. It was Zamorna. He had come up the fields by the same path as I had and, my attention being absorbed in listening to Fitz-Arthur, I had not noticed his approach. Miss Laury rose quietly up; she did not seem at all fluttered or discomposed. Ernest, with an exclamation of joy, sprang into his father's arms.

'How did you come, Papa?' said he. 'We came here to watch for you. I thought your plume would mark you from the other travellers on the valley road and now after all you've slipped our notice.'

'Slipped your notice, sir! And no wonder when you were engaged in popping the question to that black-eyed lady! Pray, how has she received the offer of your hand, heart and earldom? She does not blush; that's a bad sign.'

'I did not offer her my hand, heart and earldom, Papa, I only said I would marry her twenty years hence.'

'Tut, tut, very slack work for so early a courtship! You should have proposed tomorrow and got old Gonsalvi to knit the knot as fast as our Holy Mother Church would allow. Remember, Edward, faint heart never won fair lady[34].'

'Yes, I'll remember. I remember all you tell me, and generally say it afterwards when I've got an opportunity.'

'I'll be sworn you do! And so, where's Emily?'

'There, Papa, struggling to get to you like a little wild cat.'

'I meant *my* Emily, your mother, sir. But come, you small female imp – what eyes the child has. They are more startling than yours, Edward. Little antelope, don't flash them out of your head, for heaven's sake!'

He kissed his tiny image with paternal fondness, and then, still holding her in his arms, flung himself on the grass, and while she sat on his breast, Edward rolled about him shouting and screaming with glee as his young father sometimes pushed him off, sometimes held him in a tight grasp, and nearly killed him with laughter and tickling. Meantime two large dogs came bounding from the house, up the slope. Then there was a revival of noise and play. They rushed onto their master, whining, yelping, shaking their steel collars and padlocks, licked his face and his hands unchecked, nearly worried little Emily in their gentle yet overwhelming caresses, and buried Fitz-Arthur under the large heads and dewlap ears which they laid over his face. Zamorna encouraged them by voice and hand till at last they absolutely howled with joy; their yells, I am sure, could be heard from the distant North Road, and so could the Duke's 'Ha! Ha!', sometimes smothered when the hounds' tongues were brandishing about his mouth, and sometimes bursting forth in its full cordial clearness of sound.

What would the Angrians have thought could they have

seen their young monarch as I saw him! Many of them, I have no doubt, were then passing in the wide highway, whence came that incessant roll of wheels, almost like the rush of many waters, and continued trotting click, click of horse hooves which marks the proximity of a great city. At length the toll of a silver-voiced bell arose from the hollow.

'Bravo!' shouted Zamorna. 'Sirius! Condor! Edward! Let us see who will be at the villa vestibule first! Here, Miss Laury, take my blossom.'

He flung his daughter to Mina, and off they sprung, father, son and deerhounds, like forms of living lightning. They dived into the wood; the boughs seemed to shiver as they passed among them. In an instant they emerged on the other side, crossed the sunny, golden lawn swift as eagles; the marble portico received them and they vanished.

And now I left my station, dropped from an overhanging bough of the beech tree like a squirrel, flew down the hill as lightly as any of them, passing Miss Laury in my rapid descent like a meteor, and was at the door five minutes after them.

Zamorna was still in the entrance hall giving some orders to a servant. As he dismissed him, I came forward. His quick eye instantly caught me.

'Charles, come hither,' said he, but I edged away from him, rather afraid of the colour which was just then mounted to his face. 'Curse you!' said he, striding towards me. 'What are you afraid of? I saw you eavesdropping on the stile, and if I didn't knock your brains out then, why should I now?'

'For no mortal reason on earth, Arthur,' said I. 'And I hope you'll be civil to a gentleman in your own house and dole out a crumb or two of breakfast for the benefit of his appetite.'

He was stooping down looking at me very earnestly and his face was nearly in contact with mine. I kissed him, the first time I have ventured to do so for many a long year. He drew himself up directly, passed his hands across his lips as though my touch had defiled them, smiling, however, not ill-naturedly at the same time.

'Small monkey,' said he, 'your prying eyes cannot do much harm now, so it does not matter where you go. But, sir, had I found you here a week since I would have trod you to death on the spot.'

'Very likely,' said I, and with much inward satisfaction, for my curiosity was hissing at white heat.

I followed his imperial stride as he led towards the penetralia of the mansion. Open he flung the folding doors of one apartment in his ordinary peremptory all-commanding manner. The usual sweet scent of palace saloons mingled with the cool wildflower fragrance of a dewy summer morning and saluted my gratified nostrils as we stepped into a large and lofty room surrounded by long windows, all open, all admitting the breath and light of rising day onto Persian carpets, alabaster vases filled with flowers, velvet hangings heavily waving in the faint, fanning air, and the other splendours of taste, wealth and aristocracy.

A lady rose to welcome us. A lovely creature, she seemed the very flower of patrician beauty, with her slight but stately figure, her fair features rounded off in curves so exquisitely delicate, her marble neck so queenly and swan-like, which a small ruff turned back showed to fine advantage, her full, dark, liquid blue eye, her wreathed, braided, curled and clustered tresses whose bright abundance would scarcely be confined by the slender gold chains wound amongst them, and above all her winning, fascinating, enchanting smile.

'Mary Stuart, Mary Stuart,' muttered I in my delight and astonishment. 'A noble likeness, a dazzling eidolon! But, in the name of heaven, how is that vision connected with Zamorna?'

'Well, my Catholic Emily,' said he, as they clasped hands and joined lips, 'here I am, your own, without disguise, without concealment. All is over. Tonight the full revelation will be made, and the coronet that has long been hovering over you shall descend on that beautiful, that high-born brow.'

'I care not for that,' said she. 'I never pined after emancipation for my own sake, it was for yours. And now, if you are happy, if you feel pleasure in the unloosing of the bond, so do I. But come, you have been up all night, I dare say. This evening for severer thought, but now to breakfast. Harriet, you will attend. Blanche may go to Miss Laury; I see her coming with Gazelle. Do you know, my lord, I have given that oriental name to little Emily? Your eyes, under her eyebrows, have such a wild, flashing, eastern loveliness.'

The Duke smiled and threw himself by Mary Stuart's side as she sat down on a sofa near the window.

While they were sitting together I passed behind and whispered in Zamorna's ear, 'Poor Henrietta,' for my mind was horribly misgiving me.

'Poor Henrietta!' repeated he, not at all moved by the intimation. 'Aye, she would knit her little brows if she saw me now, and look so sad, so sorrowful, so imploring, and lift up that extraordinary face of hers to mine, with its small ivory nose and commanding, open forehead, and deep, gold curls. And then the hazel eyes would shine through such a storm of tears, and she would take my hand in her fairy palms and sob and moan as if her heart was breaking. But that would not do, would it, Emily? It's well, I think, that Finic parted us once or twice, or else I could hardly have kept up my stoicism, though I felt more inclined to laugh than anything else. So, chase away that jealous cloud, my royal lily, and look cheerful again. Your smile, you know, I have often told you, is the talisman that binds my heart and thine in the same fillet.'

'Then you shall have it,' replied the lady, smiling most sweetly. 'And I trust its power is real and not fictitious, for to speak truth, I am half afraid of that pretty, singular little girl who answered me so haughtily, and assumed such proud, passionate airs with all her childish delicacy of appearance. But look, my lord,' she said, starting, 'there are your guests coming up the lawn. That is Edward, I am sure, so like his sister, but he has blue eyes, hers are brown; see, his very hand as he lifts it to his forehead has just the white slender aspect of hers. And the other gentleman must be Fidena – proud, grave, inexorable prince; if I were not your wife I should condescend to dread his approach.'

'By the Genii,' said Zamorna, with a low and meaning laugh, 'he does look prodigiously just, immensely rigid this morning. Ho! John, I say come hither, and you, Edward, turn your righteous footsteps from the straight path to the lateral direction of this window.'

They advanced: Edward, with rapid and impatient steps, John, more slowly. Both entered through the long low casement, and stood in the presence of Zamorna and the strange lady. The Duke looked like a giant, a handsome one, but still a true indisputable Lucifer in the flesh. Something exceedingly sly, dark, secret and imperturbable lurked in the glance of his eye, the curl of his lip, and the whole cast of his grand countenance. Fidena regarded him calmly and steadily; Edward, with a fiery eagerness that seemed to show he was prepared for contest on the slightest opening. My brother spoke first.

'Well, gentlemen,' said he, 'I am obliged to your compliance with my wishes. Allow me to introduce to you Emily Inez

Wellesley, my relation in the nearest and dearest sense of the word.'

'Your wife or sister, Arthur?' asked Fidena.

'His wife to be sure,' said Edward Percy, with a bitter sneer. 'He has provided himself with one for every day in the week, like a case of razors.'

'Edward is right,' returned Zamorna, bowing with mock civility, 'this lady is my wife.'

Fidena sat down. He leant his brow on his hand a moment, but soon looked up and said very quietly, 'Well, Adrian, and is this the intelligence you had to communicate to us? I am sorry for your fickleness of disposition, which seems, in my opinion, to border on insanity, and certainly leads you to acts marked with the stain of extreme cruelty. You have committed murder once, my young friend. I should think your feelings after that flower withered at your feet were not so enviable as to make you anxious for their revival.'

'I know what you mean, John,' replied Zamorna, with equal calmness. 'You allude to Marian. She was a sweet snowdrop, but be assured – most dignified of modern Solons[35] – it was no frost of mine that blighted *her* leaves.'

'No, no,' interrupted Mr Percy. 'She died of consumption, you know, and I suppose Mary is to walk off stage in the same way, though she will be more likely – if my notions of her disposition are correct, and I should like to see who dare contradict them – to draw a knife either across her own throat or some other person's.'

'How long has that lady borne your name?' continued Fidena. 'Is the right of precedency due to the Princess Florence, the Princess Henrietta, or the Princess Inez?'

'Emily is the Chief Sultana,' answered Arthur. 'She has carried the poniard at her girdle five years, young as she looks and is. But I need say no more; here comes a noble witness to prove my affirmation.' Just then entered Fitz-Arthur. He walked towards his father.

'Edward, whose son are you?'

'Yours and Mama's,' pointing to the lady.

'That's well. And how old are you?'

'Four years.'

'Good again. Now, gentlemen, what do you say to that testimony?'

'I say that you are a scoundrel,' replied Mr Percy, 'a selfish and infernal profligate. Why did we never know of this before? Why was my sister crowned Queen of Angria when there was one who had a prior right? Why, since you kept it a secret for a lustrum, did you not keep it a secret for a century? Zamorna, this matter shall not pass unchallenged! I tell you plainly, sir, I won't be cut out from the prospect of being uncle to a future king without a struggle. You shall have a fiery furnace to go through before this lady can establish her claim of precedency. Look to it! I warn you and I defy you!'

'I must say,' remarked Fidena, 'a more unprincipled and dishonourable transaction was never brought to light within my remembrance! Adrian Wellesley, I am deeply grieved for you. You have chosen to walk in paths of darkest treachery and crime. You have acted even meanly. Your own snares are now closing you in on every side. I see nothing but shadows and dangers and universal upbraiding in the course stretching before you. The evils of a disputed succession, the horrors of internal conflict will form your legacy to Angria. You have brewed a bitter cup. Now, go, and drink it to the very dregs!'

'Well done!' exclaimed Zamorna, laughing. 'Bravo! Noble! Oh, for a legion of Cossacks to applaud the judgement of Rhadamanthus[36]! Joachim says the hurrah of the northern hordes was the grandest sound to which his ears ever tingled, but I think it could scarce do justice to that wise, good, well-considered sentence of deserved condemnation. Shall I call thee Solon or Draco[37], John? Thou art bloody minded, I think. And thou, too, our young Jupiter; denounce vengeance, hurl thy thunderbolts, bind Prometheus to the rock, transfix him with barbed lightnings, and get the insatiable vulture to gnaw the irradicable liver![38] Ha! Ha! Ha! Pity, Emily, they don't know how their fulminations are wasted. Rhadamanthus, thou art on thy throne in Tartarus[39], but the wailing wicked are all gone. No criminal stands waiting thy decree. The Furies[40] have flown, each on her awful errand; the hiss of their snakes, the yell of the tortured sounds from a vast and dreary distance, no voice save that mutters through the silence of Hades. Judge, thou art alone. Rest, then, from thy denouncing office if it be but for a moment. And, Jupiter, cease to shake Olympus with thy thunders. No one hears, no one regards them. Gods and demigods – if such a mere mortal as I might presume to dictate – let us appease our raging appetites before we go further in the matter now before us. Cities as well as men are often more savage when hungry than when full. Hebe[41], perform thine office! The mouths of the celestials water for their ethereal food – bless me, child, dost not understand? Well, then, to descend from our heroics: Harriet, my girl, hand the coffee.'

He was instantly obeyed by a young and richly dressed lady who waited in the saloon. She gracefully presented the required beverage in china cups, ornamented with gold filigree. During breakfast, an almost unbroken silence was maintained. Zamorna leant back in the sofa, regarding his two guests with a smile of the most strange and inscrutable significance. It was such as one might suppose a man might assume when on the eve of accomplishing a grand piece of gullery on an extended scale.

I think that was Mr Percy's opinion, for he suddenly rose, put down his coffee cup and approaching the Duke said, with a peculiar glance, 'My good brother-in-law, take care, if you are playing off some capital, practical joke on me! I take the liberty of informing you that your father's son is a consummate idiot. As I have a natural antipathy to jests, and he who attempts to force them down my throat generally pays a heavy penalty for his folly, be on your guard! This business wears a black face at present. If the Ethiop is not quickly washed white, I'll dye him red with the nectareous blood of your godship.'

'Eat your breakfast, Edward,' replied Zamorna. 'Here, Harriet, more nectar, more ambrosia. Jupiter Tonans[42] begins to mutter the moment his supplies fail. Rhadamanthus, now, is more exemplary. I trust his judicial bile is, by this time, diluted by streams of ameliorating chocolate.'

The meal was soon over. When it was concluded my brother rose. 'Come,' said he, 'I move that the court do adjourn into the open air. Percy, Fidena, follow me into the park, and we will see whether Edward's skill can succeed in bleaching the hide of this most swart and sunburnt Negro.'

He strode over the low window sill. His guests followed him. I thought, as the trio moved away, three finer specimens of mortality had never before stood under the sun's eye on any given square yard of our planet's surface. I watched them till they vanished amongst the thickening girdle of tall trees by which the pleasure grounds were circled. Then I turned from the window. In about an hour's time the Duke returned alone.

'Well, Emily,' said he, 'they are gone. I have convinced them. We shall meet again this evening at Waterloo Palace. You will find them ready enough to acknowledge your royal rights then. I had most difficulty with Edward. His dread of a joke is perfectly laughable, but his impetuosity is dangerous, and his incredulity unmanageable. I don't know whether I should have succeeded had not *he* arrived most opportunely. We saw him riding through the park at a distance, and as we stood on the hill I beckoned to him. Up he came, his hand on his breast, agitatedly touching the chain and miniature, and his face alternately flushed and colourless. There was no withstanding that. Fidena grasped my hand, and Edward said, with a smile, "It was well I had not jested, for, though the reality was bad enough, a joke would have been more than the value of my life." '

'And were they *fully* satisfied then?' said the lady. 'But indeed I need not ask you. They *must* have been, and now where is *he*?'

'Gone back to the city, love, with John and Percy, so we will waive the subject till evening.

'Charles,' turning to me, 'at nine o'clock *post meridian* your presence will be tolerated at Waterloo Palace. Now leave this room. I am tired of seeing your vile inquisitive looks. Trudge this instant, I say.'

Having no alternative I was forced to obey, which I did with a very bad grace. However, I solaced myself by repeating, 'nine o'clock, nine o'clock', and so strove to quiet my curiosity by anticipation, as a man endeavours to appease the calls of hunger by chewing tobacco. My efforts were as futile in the one case, as they are generally in the other.

CHAPTER EIGHT

I believe General Thornton will never forget that day. The trials of Job[43] were nothing to what he suffered during its slow, hideous, leaden progress. A thousand times did I beg him to pull out his watch and tell me the hour. Ten thousand times did I run to the door, open, look out, and then shut it. Towards night my impatience became uncontrollable. I rolled on the carpet, gnawed the fringe of the rug, screamed, kicked, and, when he attempted to chasten me with the little stick he keeps beside him for that express purpose, I seized it in my teeth and fairly bit it in two.

At last, nine o'clock found me at the vestibule of Waterloo Palace. I çrossed the entrance hall and ascended the stairs, following the train of footmen who were stationed at due distances on the landing places, etc. I entered the north drawing room. It was lit up and filled with company. A single glance sufficed to inform me that the company was all composed of the members of our own, the Fidena, and the Percy family. My Aunt Seymour seemed to be the prima donna of the evening. She occupied the principal seat, and her gentle countenance and mild unfurrowed brow, with its fair hair parted simply on each side, wore a look of calm and subdued gladness which it did my heart good to gaze on. Every now and then she glanced at her children, who sat in a group not far off. And when her eye turned on them, it filled instantly with a mingled light of maternal love, pride, and carefulness. In the midst of my cousins Seymour I saw William Percy. He was lying on an ottoman at the feet of the three eldest girls, Eliza and Georgiana and Cecillia. And the younger ones were clustered on the carpet round him, little Helen with her head resting on his knee, and her face raised smiling to his as he passed his hand caressingly through her thick brown curls. How his handsome countenance sparkled with animation! How his fine blue eyes filled with happiness and spirit and intellect as he conversed with those fair and noble daughters of that order from which rank, black, unnatural injustice alone excluded him and his more celebrated and powerful brother! I thought he devoted himself with more exclusive assiduity to Lady Cecillia Seymour than to the others, and she, I am sure, was wholly taken up with the elegant young merchant at her feet.

Cecillia is a pretty, delicate girl of mild manners and cultivated mind, very fair complexioned like her mother, not above middle size and slighter in stature than Eliza and Georgiana, who are tall haughty blondes, proud of their beauty, proud of their first-rate accomplishments, proud of their lofty lineage, proud of their semi-royal blood, proud of everything.

I was near enough to the group to hear a little of their conversation. My elder cousins indulged themselves as usual in several lively dashing sallies, which William parried and returned with great promptitude and politeness. But it was only in answer to the low yet sweet and cheerful voice of Cecillia that he kindled to the full exertion of his powers, and then eye, cheek, brow and voice were alike ardent, alike eloquent. I never heard him speak so much before, and I never heard anyone speak more animatedly and well. His talents and acquirements are little known because he is seldom seen except in the company of Edward. And Young Rogue's imposing and fiery beauty, overbearing demeanour, omnipotent abilities, athletic strength of arm and invincible soundness of lungs are more than sufficient to dash a stronger and fiercer man than William. When that Lord of the Ascendant is absent, he shines as the moon does at the going down of the sun; in his presence, he is scarcely visible.

But to proceed with a more general account of the company. Near the fireplace appeared two fine representatives of croaking and narrative old age. The Marquis Wellesley and Earl Seymour sat on the same sofa; their gouty feet on footstools, their crutches laid beside them. I need say no more. It was an impressive scene. Opposite stood a noble contrast, Edward Percy, in all his glory, surrounded by a brilliant ring of ladies, viz., Julia Sydney, the Marchioness Louisa, his own bright, dazzling Maria, the stern Countess Zenobia – for a shadow of appalling sternness did indeed dwell on her rich Italian features as she looked at her husband's disowned and detested son – the sweet Queen of Angria, who gazed at her brother as if she could not help loving him, yet feared to show her affection, the gentle Duchess of Fidena, with Rossendale at her knee looking as bold and princely as usual. And last not least, Lady Helen Percy, as grand in her declining as she could have been lovely in her ripening years.

Edward was talking with his accustomed energy and eloquence. He never paused in his flow of speech, never seemed at a loss for a word, but went on warming and kindling as he proceeded, his voice not boisterously high but by no means inaudibly low. His hand every now and then raised and pushed amongst the clusters of his gold-streaked auburn ringlets, which he thrust from his forehead as if he could not bear that the intrusion of a single lock should darken its ample alabaster expanse.

At a distance from these and seated in separate recesses, I saw two groups whose appearance somewhat astonished me. One consisted of the lady of Douro Villa, her children and their governess, Mina Laury; the other of a figure which looked startlingly like the late Marchioness of Douro. She was attired in black velvet, her snow-white arms and neck were uncovered and seemed most brilliantly fair when opposed to the sable folds of her dress. A little girl stood at the back of her chair, and beside her sat a tall gentleman in a half military blue surtout, black stock and white pantaloons. It was Lady Frances Millicent Hume, her protégée, Euphemia Lindsay, and His Grace, the Duke of Fidena. Surely, thought I, this must be an important family affair which has caused that sightless bird to be summoned from her sequestered bower in Alderwood. I could see her lips move as she sat, but her voice was too low to reach my ear. Fidena bent over her so kindly and tenderly and bowed his stately head to listen when she spoke, and answered her with such condescending gentleness that more than one grateful tear stole from under her closed lids and down her pallid cheek, and from thence dropped like a diamond on her dress. Yet she appeared serene and happy. Such were the company assembled within the gilded and pictured walls of the north drawing room at Waterloo Palace. Three were wanting to complete the tale, and for these I looked in vain. The Duke of Wellington, the Earl of Northangerland, and the King of Angria were absent. At length the former entered. All rose to salute him.

'Well,' said he, regarding them with his cordial glance and smile, 'how are you all? I hope well. It was my intention to have been with you before now, but I was detained by His Lordship of Northangerland. Mr Percy, your father would not breathe under the same ceiling with you, so I have been forced to explain to him the matter which has brought you together in my library. He is digesting it now at his leisure and in a few minutes you shall be favoured with the like information. Now sit down and wait quietly if you can.'

He then went round, addressing a few words more particularly to each. 'Well, Emily, are you pretty well this evening? So, Millicent, having a little conversation with Fidena, I see. Aye, Julia, don't burst with curiosity, you look as if you could hardly live out the next five minutes. Louisa, you actually seem awake tonight.'

'I am longing for a sight of Zamorna,' said she.

'He will come soon,' replied my father.

'Where is he? Where is he?' asked several of the ladies Seymour at once.

'Silence, you girls!' observed Fitzroy. 'I say, Uncle, what's become of my cousin?'

Many now gathered round where the Duke stood, all, in fact, except Emily, Millicent, Edward Percy, the Duke of Fidena and the Countess Seymour. Amidst the confusion of question, reply, conjecture, anticipation, apprehension, etc., etc., I, who was standing near the door listening impatiently for approaching footsteps, heard a tread. At first it sounded only as of one person but as it drew nigher the steps of two were distinctly audible. The folding doors moved a little, then there was a pause, a low and earnest whispering of voices. Again the handle turned, the portals noiselessly expanded, and two gentlemen of very lofty stature, bowing their heads slightly under the arch, crossed the threshold of the saloon. They walked towards the upper end, unobserved by any save me, and the few, above mentioned, who had not joined the general group, and placed themselves side by side near the mantelpiece. Both looked round a moment, then took off their military caps, and, turning to each other, burst into a loud and ringing laugh.

All turned as simultaneously as if the same soul had actuated each individual body. A dead stony silence succeeded the smothered rustle which this movement occasioned, but soon I heard a quick, hurried, throbbing pulsation of hearts, and saw the blood rushing to some cheeks, and fading away from others till it left them white as death.

Amongst the latter was the Queen of Angria. She leant against the wall. Her eyes grew so fixed and glazed that they lost all expression, and seemed as soulless as those of a corpse; her lips parted; a damp perspiration began to glisten on her forehead. Well might she be shocked, stunned, astounded; well might all present be petrified and struck speechless.

Standing erect on the hearth, with the full flow of a blazing chandelier streaming radiantly on him and revealing every feature as distinctly as if a ray of sunlight had marked him like an index, appeared the Duke of Zamorna, the monarch of Angria. And near at hand, so that it seemed almost to touch him, equally illuminated by that amber lustre, just as distinctly seen, just as clearly defined, appeared his wraith! For by no other name can I term that awful vision which stood beside him face to face – so like in every lineament, limb and motion that none could tell which was the substance, which the shadow. Flesh and spirit glanced at each other, solemnly sundered; eye flashed to eye, lip curled to lip, brow darkened to brow, each refulgent head lifted to such a haughty and equal altitude, it seemed as if, of all the brown, crimson-lit curls that crowded in such bright and glossy beauty on their temples, not one could boast a hair more or less than the other. There was a universal shock given to every spectator as one of them, advancing a step forward and bowing with cool military grace, said with a lit and laughing eye, 'Sons and daughters of the race of Wellesley, of Percy, of Fidena, you have all known

Arthur Augustus Adrian Wellesley, Duke of Zamorna and Marquis of Douro and King of Angria, long; admit to your acquaintance his twin brother Ernest Julius Mornington Wellesley, Duke of Valdacella, Marquis of Alhama and heir apparent of Wellingtonsland.

I cannot describe the scene that followed; I cannot even recollect it distinctly. My senses seemed bewildered. There was a rush towards the hearth, a burst of exclamations, a sudden outstretching of hands, a sound of greeting and welcome, above which arose the wild, mingled laugh of the simulacra like a trumpet swell over the roar of a cataract. It subsided soon and then I could look around me.

Mary was standing before them, gazing alternately at each with a look of agitated and puzzled yet pleasurable emotion. She was not left long in doubt. One of them caught her suddenly in his arms, and, as she sank sobbing on his breast, I heard her murmur, 'Then Zamorna is all my own! He has ever loved me! Finic did only his duty! *Can* I, oh, Adrian, *dare* I hope for forgiveness?'

He silently pressed his lips to her forehead, and she, recollecting that many eyes were on them, blushingly turned away her face and, struggling from him, retired to a recess where she sat down as happy as renewed confidence in her lord's love and fealty could make her. Valdacella, as I must call my new-found brother, followed his sister-in-law with his eyes; a keen ironical smile began to dimple the corners of his mouth. He walked up to Miss Laury and, taking from her the little gazelle-like creature she held in her lap, stepped with it to the Duchess.

'Ahem,' said he, elevating his arched brows. 'You once said this little girl was very, very like her unworthy father, and said it too with a deep-drawn and most grievous sigh. I recollect I,

116

like a prophet, foretold a time should come when you would not sorrow for that likeness. Is it come now, Henrietta? Say yes, or I'll never forgive you!'

'Indeed, but it is!' returned the Duchess, snatching the bright bud of beauty from him and kissing it warmly. 'I love little Emily now all the better for her large Zamornian orbs.'

'Valdacellian, rather you should say,' returned he. 'But here is another coming to claim your regard.'

At that moment Ernest ran up. 'Papa, Papa!' said he. 'May I call you Papa now before other people? May I call Zamorna uncle? And may this lady go with us to Castle Oronsay? For she seems good and has left off crying and I dare say she's sorry for having been angry with Mama.'

His father smiled and, turning away, went back to the main cluster of guests. I followed him.

'Brother,' said I, 'you have not yet spoken to me. Was it not yourself who knocked me down in the carriage when we were returning from Almeida's funeral?'

He replied by taking my hand in his and squeezing with that gentle, insinuating pressure which had, at the time, so awakened my curiosity.

'Dear, dear Ernest,' said I, 'I think I shall love you far better than Arthur.'

He curled his lip and pushed me scornfully off.

And now the demand for explanation, immediate and satisfactory explanation of all the strange, and, as yet, undeveloped mystery began to grow loud and peremptory. Cousins, aunts, uncles etc., thronged about the Gemini overwhelming them with a hundred questions: 'Why had the secret been kept so long? Why had it been kept at all? Who was the Duchess of Valdacella? Where had she and her husband been living? etc., etc., etc.'

'For heaven's sake have mercy on us!' exclaimed Zamorna. 'If you will be silent, I'll tell you all I am able. Perfect satisfaction I cannot promise, but such as I have, give I unto you. Form a ring. Georgiana and Eliza, stand back, and you, Julius, leave off playing the fool with those little ones there. Helen, come to my side. Cecillia, go to William Percy; nay, you need not blush. I mean nothing particular. Millicent, love, no one seems to be caring for you; take this seat near my aunt. Julius – curse you, get out of my way! And you too, Edward Percy! No hectoring, sir; go and bully Valdacella if you are in the humour. Effie, my fairy, look less bewildered, and put back thy yellow locks, child. Julia Sydney, Aunt Louisa, Agnes, Catherine, Fitzroy, Maria, Lily, my Empress Zenobia – one and all of you – retreat.'

When something like order and silence was restored, he commenced giving the following brief outline of explanation, leaning against the mantelpiece while he spoke, with Valdacella sitting near him and watching sharply for an opportunity to correct or add or deduct as the case might need it.

'On this day, precisely twenty-two years ago, my brother and I first opened our eyes on the troubles and pleasures of this world. What o'clock was it, Father?'

The Duke of Wellington smiled at this appeal from his tall young giant of a son, while another of equal stature at the same moment turned enquiringly to him.

'It was,' he replied, 'just five minutes past nine o'clock p.m. of the eighteenth of July 1812, that a pair of young gentlemen, who were destined severally and unitedly to give the world assurance of a scoundrel, were presented to me under the title of Prince of Wellingtonsland.'

'Humph!' said Zamorna, and went on. 'Well, it so happened

that Julius here, with the effrontery that marks his character, chose to take precedence of me. By a very fraction of time certainly, but sufficient to entitle him to the birthright. Like an Esau, as he is, though I am no Jacob, yet, had my mother been a Rebecca and my father an Isaac, I would have been a willing supplanter.'[44]

'Curse you, nobody doubts that!' interrupted Valdacella. 'Get on faster or I'll take the reins out of your hands! In fact, I will without delay. Ladies and gentlemen,' he continued, rising, 'being born, we were as like as peas; having snub noses of precisely the same dimensions, saucer eyes of equal circumference, squalling mouths each of the same cherry shape and colour.'

'I'll make yours of a redder colour and a totally nondescript shape presently,' said Zamorna, endeavouring to push Valdacella back into his seat. Julius, however, struggled against him, and a regular wrestling match ensued.

'Tiger cubs!' said my father, half-amused and half-angry. 'You are neither of you fit to speak three consecutive words in the presence of a Christian assembly. Isabella, part them while I finished the explanation they've scarcely commenced. As one of them (I don't know which) said, they were each mere repetitions of the other from the moment of their birth, so that the women who took care of them could not tell the difference any more than the women who now take care of them will be able to do. The instant after they were brought into the world, a tremendous storm broke over the town and Palace of Mornington, and indeed over all Wellingtonsland from one end to the other. I remember a flash of lightning glanced suddenly over their faces when I first looked at them, and, instead of screaming, they opened their large eyes, knit their diminutive brows, and seemed angrily and impudently to defy it. Throughout the night, wind, thunder and rain emulatively howled, roared, rattled and splashed amongst the great castellated heap of buildings that compose Mornington Court. For one that believed in omens, this would have been a fine subject of speculation and conjecture, but as I seldom bother my head about such matters – hah, Countess, what a frown! – I went to bed – steady, my lady – and tried to go to sleep – no crime, I trust, Zenobia – as soon as ever the bustle those fellows had occasioned in every part of the house was a little subsided.

'It was dead of night, the very witching hour, all silent, all slumbering, except the elements and probably the new-sprung scions, when a tremendous clattering knock on the great door, accompanied by a furious jangling of the bell, shook the old castle till its very foundations rocked. Presently, after I heard the challenging of sentinels, and the hurrying tread of porters, the bars were withdrawn and the unhappy and belated soul without admitted. Then came a brief period of altercation. It seemed, by the obstreperous swearing and anathemising, that the aroused menials had not found the traveller to equal the expectations raised by his pompous summons. I heard an old Scotch Yeoman, Seneschal of the Court, Jamie Lindsay by name, the father of Harry, my son's chancellor ("Hem! Ahem!") exclaim in his broad northern twang, "Kick the auld gaberlunzie[45] out, for his impidence. Wha wad think o' the likes o' him a tinker-loon, without plack or boddle,[46] knocking up them whilk are sae mickle his betters as us, Seneschals of the Court and Yeomen of the Dynasty Guard, forbye disturbing my leddy and the princes wi' his un-Christian clishma-claver[47]; kick him out, I say, and let him dee at the back o' the dyke."

'To this pitiless sentence the voice of Dennis, or as he was commonly called Dinnish Laury, ancestor of Edward Laury, sounded in audible reply: "Och, botheration, ye're not going to turn out the gintleman this a'way are ye? Not but he desarves it well for his din, and bad luck to him! But it's not them wet hard flags that any of us would choose for a bed this same night. So, be my soul, Jim, as it would sound ill to have it told that a gintleman had died afore the Duke's threshold, for want of shelter, on the very birth-night of our young lords, sure it's myself'll give him a lodging and a supper anyhow. Come along azy, you thief of the wurlt."'

'Arthur,' interrupted the Marquis Wellesley, who had been fidgeting all the while my father uttered this piece of brogue with true Hibernian accent and emphasis – assumed, I believe, on purpose to discompose his brother and the Countess of Northangerland who, I thought, would have died of the scorn and indignation which she dared not give vent to. 'Arthur, what can you mean by repeating to us the conversation of a couple of low-bred serving men? Pray get forwards with the main story.'

'Oh,' said Zenobia, 'I beg my lord you will permit your royal relative to indulge in a pleasure he can so seldom enjoy. Let the great Wellington come down from his heroic elevation of king and conqueror, and Sampson-like[48] deign to make sport before us Philistines by showing us how they talk in Ireland.'

A quiet laugh was the Duke's only answer to this bitter sarcasm. Valdacella took Zenobia's hand and, looking into her face with that bold and mischievous smile which had so distressed Mary, observed, 'Be azy, my jewel, take things calmly and comfortably, and in return let us hear, not how they talk, but how they swear, in your country. I think an oath or two would do you good.'

She turned from him in high disdain and tried to extricate her hand but he held it fast.

'No frowning!' he said. 'No airs of imperiousness! If you like Augustus, you must like me; there is no choice for it; and' – in a lower tone – 'this is not the first time I have spoken to you, and held your hand also. Often, often have words of yours, which were intended for the ear of Zamorna, been poured into that of Valdacella. And many others are in the same predicament. There is not one here, man or woman, who has not stood, sat, or walked by my side by sunlight, moonlight or candlelight, unknown to themselves, unknown indeed to the whole world but me and my twin brother, and not always to him. Fair Countess, frown, but you cannot hate me.'

'By my life, she shall hate you!' said Zamorna, who, while he spoke, had stolen softly behind him. And at the same instant he delivered him a smart box on the ear. Julius turned. They stood fronting each other. It was an edifying sight. Each face flushed, each brow bent, each lip bit, each eye filled with fierceness. So altogether alike, so undistinguishably similar. Tiger cubs, whelps of one litter, indeed, they looked. Fiercely malignant were their mutual glances for some seconds, but all at once something, probably the resemblance, appeared to strike them in a ludicrous point of view. They burst into a simultaneous laugh and, each bestowing on the other a short but energetic curse, strode to opposite parts of the room.

'Well,' said the Duke of Wellington, 'now that wise panto-mime is over I will proceed. Scarcely half an hour after the castle gates had been again closed, and when all was subsiding into quietness, a fresh bustle arose in some of the distant chambers. I listened awhile and, finding that it increased instead of diminishing, I got up and dressed myself with all possible expedition. Stepping out into the corridor I was startled by a loud shriek, and skipping down the long lamp-lit passage appeared a creature of low stature and in aspect not much unlike my sons' valets Finic and Pinic, only thinner and more agile. It flung out its arms and came on laughing, shouting and yelling most infernally. I was not long in recognising little Harry Lindsay, then about ten years old, a vile, mischievous, clever imp, who deserved horsewhipping every day of his life and every hour of that day. I asked him what was the matter, rather sternly I believe, for he shot sideways and stood at a respectful distance.

'"Come to our Minnie," said he still laughing, "my lord Duke, she's clean red-wud[49], and sae are the bairns, and sae are all the women folk. The young rottens have fastened ilk ane on the ither's trapple[50] like wull cats, and there's ane gotten amang 'em wham they cana be redd o', ane that Dinnish Laury axed ben the house. Oh come, come, dinna lose the sports, I maun away whild the door stands ajow," and off he darted as fast as lightning.

'I followed pretty quickly. The imp entered a chamber at the end of the corridor, whence the noise seemed to proceed. On crossing the threshold of the same room, a pretty scene met my eyes. It was well lit and I suppose, by the appearance of a cradle etc., had been fitted up for the nursery of those two tall gentlemen standing so sullenly apart from each other in separate recesses. In the very centre of the floor, just under the hanging lamp, I saw a pair of span-long candidates for limbo, the royal twins of that day's creation, rolling about in the convulsions of mortal hostility, one on the top of the other, struggling, screaming in short, sharp, shrill squeaks like small beasts of prey, striving with all their might and with an unnatural energy that made them appear possessed, each to strangle his brother. Close beside them stood a tall gaunt man in black, a Quaker's broad-brimmed beaver in one hand, which he shied every now and then as if instigating them to fiercer combat. His countenance was very grave and serious, and his manner as he bent over them, with his hands spread on his knees, most solemnly yet ludicrously anxious. Harry Lindsay capered about in all directions, clapping his hands, grinning with delight, and exclaiming at intervals, "Huzza! Go it, rottens, that beats cock-fetchin," etc. To complete the picture, Mrs Lindsay sat weeping, wringing her hands, and audibly lamenting without attempting to separate the champions. And in the background were three or four young girls in the same lachrymose condition.

'As soon as surprise would let me, I attempted to come to the rescue, but in vain. I found I could not get beyond a circular line of chalk, about three yards round, which was drawn upon the floor, and yet there was no visible impediment to stop me. So it was, however – doubt it who dare!

'Well, the Dowager Countess of Mornington, Lady Isabella Wellesley now Lady Seymour, Lady Isidore Hume, our friend the doctor, Sir Alexander, then rather different to what he is now, Mr Maxwell, young Edward Laury, Old Dennis, Jamie Lindsay and some others were called in, but all to no purpose. I only remember that Lindsay, who was then a stern old man, knocked down his son Harry and kicked him senseless out of the room, muttering at the same time something about the wickedness of giving way to carnal delight at a time when God's judgements were visibly upon us. At last the conflict ceased, seemingly from the exhaustion of the principal actors.

'The fellow in black then took them up, placed them in their cradle, walked several times round them, and afterwards in a loud, harsh, singing tone pronounced a sort of spell in rhyme, the purport of which was that, though two scions seemed to have sprung from the parent tree, yet, for a length of time they should in reality be but as one; for that it should henceforth be death to them to be looked upon by mortal eyes at the same time, to have even their existence known by more than twelve persons, or to live and associate with each other. He gave to one of them (Arthur, the younger by a minute or two) the privileges of name, fame and existence, adding thereto the penalties consequent on discovery. Ernest he exempted from these, but condemned him to retirement and obscurity. He concluded by declaring that the spell should never be unloosed till the ripe fruit of the opening bud had fallen, till the gift and the giver were both departed. So saying he pulled a black card-case from his pocket, opened it, took out a card, threw in on the table, and with a low bow left the room. The card was like any ordinary note of address and bore these words: *Henri Nicolai, Flesher and Spirit Merchant, Styx-wharf, Close by the Gates of Hades – 18th July – Cycle of Eternity.*

'From that day to this the spell has wrought strongly and efficiently. Nicolai returned at times and renewed it. No human power could avail to counteract his machinations, and the consequence has been what you all see. Alhama was wholly unknown but by no means wholly unknowing. He has been nearly as much in the society of those here present and in that of the other inhabitants of Verdopolis as his brother Douro. Their past lives are inextricably interwoven; the achievements of one cannot now be distinguished from the achievements of the other; their writings, their military actions, their political manoeuvres are all blended, all twisted into the same cord, a cord which none but themselves can unravel and which they will not. Even the sins, incidents, and adventures of their private life are so confused and mingled that it would require a sharp eye to discover what lies to the charge of Zamorna and what to that of Valdacella. They often quarrel with, because they often cross, each other, yet the sympathy and similarity between their minds and persons is so great that, upon the whole, they agree much better than for the convenience of society it could be wished they did.

'I have now only to introduce my daughter-in-law, the Duchess of Valdacella, Marchioness of Alhama, and future Queen of Wellingtonsland. Come hither, Emily. She is the only child of the wealthy, aged, and patrician Duke of Morena, whose vast possessions all lie in the north of Sneachie's Land, along the shores of the Genif Sea. Ernest first saw her when he was travelling there, a boy, unattended and unknown. She was romantic; so was he. Thence, greatly to the gratification of his own vanity, when considered only as a nameless and fortuneless adventurer, he wooed and won the heiress of all the Hills. After he had secured her oath of everlasting fidelity, the young scapegrace condescended to reveal to her the splendid mystery of his birth and doom. Of course that proved a conclusive argument both with herself and father. They were married out of hand, the bridegroom being precisely eighteen on the day of his nuptials, the bride, fifteen. Emily, on the mother's side, comes of the old Roman Catholic family of the Ravenswoods and is herself a devout daughter of Holy Kirk. Since her marriage she has resided at Castle Oronsay, situated in the centre of Loch Sunart, ten miles from the town of Kinrira and not far from Ben Carnach, which, with the lands round it, she laid at the feet of her royal husband as a dowry on their wedding day. There she has the pleasure of his company about six months out of the twelve, not more, I am certain, the rest of his time having been devoted to playing the fool and the knave with his scoundrel colleague in Verdopolis, etc. They have two children, Ernest Edward Ravenswood Wellesley, Earl Ravenswood and Viscount Mornington, and

Lady Emily Augusta Wellesley who will be bred up a little worshipper of the Virgin, I presume. Now I have done. Cross-question them as you like.'

As the Duke concluded, Valdacella started up.

'Men, women and children,' said he, 'I insist upon it that you do not treat me as a stranger. I know you all, body, mind and estate. Julia, don't look incredulous; I have laughed and talked with thee for hours, almost for days together. Edward Percy, thou knowest that I know thee; so dost thou, sister Henrietta; Georgiana and Eliza, no need of your assumed reserves, I have your proud hearts in my hand. Zenobia, you have as often studied the ancients and devoured the moderns with Julius as with Augustus. My Lady of Fidena, I was the acquaintance of Lily Hart and not Zamorna. Millicent, Oramare is certainly Zamorna's and so is Alderwood, and he married his Florence the year after I married my Inez. But for all that, Ernest's hand has often led and guided your happiness, spending a day with you at Alnwick Castle scarcely a month since. Aunt Louisa, Julius has teased you as often as Arthur. Maria, Douro and Alhama are as one; since your marriage you have promised to be my sister, and before that Zamorna was not more frequently your Ilderim than I was. Tell Edith she lectured me with her gentle voice and solemn eyes last night. Tell Arundel, he gave an oath of friendship to me written in his own blood. By heaven, you shall receive me as an old, long-tried associate or I'll make some of you repent it.' He ceased.

They all declared their readiness to acquiesce at once in his wishes, and amidst the renewed bustle of congratulations, surprise and pleasure, I beg leave to drop the curtain.

PS A novel can scarcely be called a novel unless it ends in a marriage, therefore I herewith tack to, add and communicate the following *postscriptum* which may perhaps be pronounced the only real piece of information contained in the book.

Yesterday married in St Augustin's Cathedral by the Right Revd Dr Stanhope, Primate of all Angria, Captain William Percy of the Royal Life Guards of Angria and aide-de-camp to His Grace the Duke of Zamorna, to Lady Cecillia, daughter of Earl Seymour and niece to the Duke of Wellington. We understand the monarch of Wellingtonsland, to testify his approbation of the bridegroom's conduct in quitting a commercial for a military life, presented him after the ceremony with a cheque for one hundred thousand pounds. The bride's dowry amounted to eighty thousand pounds, in addition to which she will shortly come into possession of an estate of nearly three thousand a year left her by her uncle the late Colonel Vavasour Seymour, whose favourite niece she was. We have not heard what share of profits the celebrated young eastern merchant Mr Percy has allowed as his brother's share. It is said on the Exchange that Young Rogue declared openly, the clerk's salary should be punctually paid but not a stiver[51] more.

Vale, Reader, Cecillia Seymour and William Percy make a fair and loving couple. Here's health, wealth, happiness and long life to them.

Reader, I am thine,

C.A.F. Wellesley

NB I think I have redeemed my pledge. I think I have proved the Duke of Zamorna to be partially insane by a circuitous and ambiguous road certainly, but still by one in which no traveller can be lost. Reader, if there is no Valdacella there ought to be one. If the young King of Angria has no alter ego he ought to have such a convenient representative, for no single man, having one corporeal and one spiritual nature, if these were rightly compounded without any mixture of pestilential ingredients, should, in right reason and in the ordinance of common sense and decency, speak and act in that capricious, double-dealing, unfathomable, incomprehensible, torturing, sphinx-like manner which he constantly assumes for reasons known only to himself. I say, my brother has too many reins in his hands, believe me or understand me who will. He has gathered the symbols of dominion in a mighty grasp; he strains all the energy, all the power, all the talent of his soul to retain them; he struggles, he ponders, night and day, morning and evening, to hold the empire he has established in so many lands, so many hearts, so many interests. He strives to keep them under one rule and government and to prevent them, if possible, from coming into collision. His brain throbs, his blood boils, when they wince and grow restive under his control, which they often do, for should they once break loose, should the talisman of his influence once fail –! Mighty Genii, draw a veil over the scene! There is a sound, a stun, a crash, a smothered but deep, dull, desperate peal of thunder heard amidst the volumed fold of clouds which hide and pervade futurity. But further I dare not look, more I dare not hear.

Reader, what say you to the image of a crowned maniac, dying dethroned, forsaken, desolate, in the shrieking gloom of a madhouse. No light around him but the discoloured beam which falls through grated windows on scattered straw, his kingdom gone, his crown a mockery, those who worshipped him dead or estranged: 'All earth a dreary void to him / All heaven a cloud of gloom.'[52]

Oh, Zamorna! think not of the field of battle, think not of the trampling of horses and garments rolled in blood, nor of the deathbed amidst piles of slain, with 'Victory' for the last sound lingering in thine ear, and a song of triumph for thy burial hymn. Trumpets may pour the dirge for the captains of thine armies, 'Arise' may be their battle shout, and thy sun their exalting standard,[53] while thou art mouldering in earth, utterly forgotten or remembered only to be despised – Zamorna, a young man of promise. He attempted, however, more than he could perform; his affairs grew embarrassed and perplexed; he became insane and died in a private madhouse at the early age of twenty-two.

C. Brontë

NOTES

1. Lord Charles Albert Florian Wellesley was Charlotte Brontë's preferred pseudonym throughout her juvenilia.

2. In the juvenilia, Verdopolis was the old federal capital, Angria the new kingdom.

3. Tadmor was a city built by Solomon in the wilderness (2 Chronicles 8: 4); the destruction of the ancient city of Tyre was prophesied in Isaiah 23.

4. Calabar, a trading state on the port of the Gulf of Guinea, grew in importance during the nineteenth century, when Charlotte Brontë was writing *The Spell*.

5. *To dree one's weird* was to suffer one's fate.

6. The words used in the 'Burial of the Dead' from *The Book of Common Prayer* (1662).

7. From Handel's *Messiah* (1742), based on the words from Job 19: 25.

8. Confuse with your hubbub (Yorkshire dialect).

9. Hearse (contemporary slang).

10. *The Confessional of the Black Crucifix* by Thomas Uwins (1782–1857).

11. In Milton's *Paradise Lost* (1667) the angel Ithuriel is charged by Gabriel to find Satan in Paradise.

12. As told by Sophocles (496–406 BC), Oedipus alone solved the riddle set by the Sphinx who guarded the entrance to Thebes.

13. Sir Francis Legatt Chantrey (1784–1841), English Sculptor famous for his busts.

14. Like Mary, Queen of Scots (1542–87), Emily Inez was both Scottish and Catholic; in *The Spell* she is frequently referred to as Mary, Queen of Scots.

15. A symbol of female authority.

16. Bully.

17. 'rings and plumes and pearls / Are shining everywhere' are lines from *Lalla Rookh: An Oriental Romance* (1817) by Thomas Moore (1779–1852).

18. The four Chief Genii were Charlotte, Branwell, Emily and Anne Brontë.

19. See Revelation 14: 15.

20. Now Kamchatka, a peninsula at the far eastern edge of Russia.

21. In Greek mythology, Atropos was one of the three Fates; her particular role was to cut off the thread of life.

22. Messalina (*c.*22–*c.*48) was the wife of Emperor Claudius of Rome (10 BC– AD 54), notorious for her sexual infidelity; it was in fact Claudius' fourth wife, Agrippina (15–49), who is believed to have poisoned him.

23. Socrates (469–399 BC), the Greek philosopher, was sentenced to death by drinking hemlock.

24. In a previous story, *High Life in Verdopolis*, Pelham had requested Mary's hand in marriage and was refused.

25. A reference to the Israelites' captivity in Egypt, recorded in Genesis and Exodus.

26. Worse (dialect).

27. The land immediately surrounding a house.

28. In Homer's *Odyssey*, Scylla, a six-headed sea monster, lived in a cave and attacked sailors, reducing them to bones. 'By the bones of Scylla' is a favourite expression of the Earl of Northangerland in the juvenilia.

29. 'My God! I'm done for' (French).

30. From *The Pilgrim's Progress: Part One* (1678) by John Bunyan (1628–88).

31. Weeping, crying, mournful (Italian).

32. Now Kandahar in Afghanistan and Isfahan in Iran.

33. A hackney-coachman.

34. A popular expression, hailing from 'And let us mind, faint heart ne'er wan / A lady fair' from 'To Dr Blacklock' by Robert Burns (1759–96).

35. Athenian statesman and lawmaker Solon (*c.*638–*c.*558 BC) was one of the Seven Sages of Greece.

36. In Greek mythology, Rhadamanthus, son of Zeus, was one of the three judges of the underworld.

37. Like Solon (see note 34), Draco of Athens (*c.*659–*c.*601 BC) was one of the Seven Sages of Ancient Greece, noted for the severity of the laws he introduced.

38. Charged by Jupiter – the supreme god of the Roman pantheon and the equivalent of Zeus in Greek mythology – to give men gifts that would ensure their survival, Prometheus bestowed the gift of fire, stolen from the gods; in punishment of this he was chained to a rock in the mountains where vultures would prey on his liver for eternity.

39. In Greek mythology, the lowest region of the world.

40. The Furies – Alecto, Megaera and Tisiphone – were winged creatures who pursued and punished doers of unavenged crimes.

41. The goddess of youth and spring, and cupbearer to the gods.

42. Jupiter Tonans: an epithet for Jupiter meaning 'Jupiter the Thunderer'.

43. See the Old Testament book of Job; despite the immense suffering inflicted on him by Satan, Job refused to curse God.

44. See Genesis 25 and 27; Esau sold his birthright to his younger brother Jacob, only for Jacob, with his mother's help, then to deceive their father Isaac into giving him his blessing.

45. Beggar (Scottish).

46. Without a farthing (Scottish).

47. Foolish talk (Scottish).

48. See Judges 15–16; Samson, leader of the Israelites, confounded the Philistines with his great strength. The spelling and context also indicate a possible reference to Domine Sampson, a character in Scott's *Guy Mannering*.

49. Mad (Scottish).

50. Windpipe (Scottish).

51. A small Dutch coin, i.e. a little bit, a small amount.

52. From *Don Juan* XIV, lxxix, l. 625, by Lord Byron (1788–1824).

53. Zamorna's banner was the image of a rising sun.

The Spell, whilst a complete story in itself, forms part of Charlotte Brontë's extensive juvenilia, much of which is set in her imagined kingdoms of Angria and Verdopolis. Although it involves the same characters that appear in other stories from the juvenilia, *The Spell* introduces a number of crucial differences that are unique to this particular work, namely the roles of Ernest Julius Mornington Wellesley, Zamorna's identical twin brother, and his family. To justify this departure from the established 'facts' of the juvenilia, Brontë devises an elaborate literary conceit – Lord Charles' premeditated exposure of Zamorna as a hypocritical tyrant. However, such deliberate obfuscation of events and characters on Brontë's part would seem to indicate that she is experimenting in her writing in an attempt to attain new heights of storytelling. The sometimes confusing, contradictory nature of the work can therefore be seen to be that of a young writer – she was, at the time of writing, only eighteen – who is wrestling with how to record a splintered personality, and whilst here she resorts to magic spells and alter egos, it is only a matter of time before she will bring her efforts to perfection in *Jane Eyre*, written some thirteen years later.

Charlotte Brontë was born in Thornton, Yorkshire, in 1816. In 1820 her father was appointed curate at Haworth and the family moved to Haworth Parsonage where Charlotte was to spend most of her life. Following the death of her mother in 1821 and of her two eldest sisters in 1825, she and her two surviving sisters, Emily and Anne, and brother, Branwell, were brought up by their father and a devoutly religious aunt.

Theirs was an unhappy childhood, in particular the period the sisters spent at a school for daughters of the clergy. Charlotte abhorred the harsh regime, blaming it for the death of her two sisters, and she went on to fictionalise her experiences there in *Jane Eyre* (1847). Having been removed from the school, the three sisters, together with Branwell, found solace in storytelling. Inspired by a set of toy soldiers, they created the imaginary kingdoms of Angria and Gondola which form the settings for much of their juvenilia. From 1831 to 1832 Charlotte was educated at Roe Head school where she later returned as a teacher.

In 1842 Charlotte travelled to Brussels with Emily. They returned home briefly following the death of their aunt, but, soon after, Charlotte was back in Brussels, this time as a teacher. At great expense, the three sisters published a volume of poetry – *Poems by Currer, Ellis and Acton Bell* (1846) – but this proved unsuccessful, selling only two copies. By the time of its publication, each of the sisters had completed a novel: Emily's *Wuthering Heights*, and Anne's *Agnes Grey* were both published in 1847, but Charlotte's novel, *The Professor*, remained unpublished in her lifetime. Undeterred, Charlotte embarked on *Jane Eyre*, which was also published in 1847 and hailed by Thackeray as 'the masterwork of a great genius'. She followed this up with *Shirley* (1849) and *Villette* (1853), and continued to be published under the pseudonym Currer Bell although her identity was, by now, well known.

Branwell, in many ways the least successful of the four siblings, died in 1848. His death deeply distressed the sisters, and both Emily and Anne died within the following year. Charlotte married her father's curate in 1854, but she died in the early stages of pregnancy in March 1855.

SELECTED TITLES FROM HESPERUS PRESS

Author	Title	Foreword writer
Pedro Antonio de Alarcón	*The Three-Cornered Hat*	
Louisa May Alcott	*Behind a Mask*	Doris Lessing
Edmondo de Amicis	*Constantinople*	Umberto Eco
Pietro Aretino	*The School of Whoredom*	Paul Bailey
Pietro Aretino	*The Secret Life of Nuns*	
Jane Austen	*Lesley Castle*	Zoë Heller
Jane Austen	*Love and Friendship*	Fay Weldon
Honoré de Balzac	*Colonel Chabert*	A.N. Wilson
Charles Baudelaire	*On Wine and Hashish*	Margaret Drabble
Aphra Behn	*The Lover's Watch*	
Giovanni Boccaccio	*Life of Dante*	A.N. Wilson
Charlotte Brontë	*The Foundling*	
Charlotte Brontë	*The Green Dwarf*	Libby Purves
Emily Brontë	*Poems of Solitude*	Helen Dunmore
Mikhail Bulgakov	*Fatal Eggs*	Doris Lessing
Mikhail Bulgakov	*A Dog's Heart*	A.S. Byatt
Giacomo Casanova	*The Duel*	Tim Parks
Miguel de Cervantes	*The Dialogue of the Dogs*	Ben Okri
Geoffrey Chaucer	*The Parliament of Birds*	
Anton Chekhov	*The Story of a Nobody*	Louis de Bernières
Anton Chekhov	*Three Years*	William Fiennes
Wilkie Collins	*The Frozen Deep*	
Wilkie Collins	*Who Killed Zebedee?*	Martin Jarvis
Arthur Conan Doyle	*The Mystery of Cloomber*	
Arthur Conan Doyle	*The Tragedy of the Korosko*	Tony Robinson
William Congreve	*Incognita*	Peter Ackroyd
Joseph Conrad	*Heart of Darkness*	A.N. Wilson
Joseph Conrad	*The Return*	Colm Tóibín
Gabriele D'Annunzio	*The Book of the Virgins*	Tim Parks